Books by Rob Hill
in the Linford Western Library:

RANGELAND JUSTICE
HOPE'S LAST CHANCE
ACE HIGH IN WILDERNESS

SHERIFF OF VENGEANCE

With a failing farm, and with nightmare memories of the war, Clay Butterfield and his wife Rose Alice abandon life in the East. They join a wagon train bound for California. However, when their departure is delayed, Clay finds out that a gunman is in town, intent on killing him. Instinct tells him to run, but to protect Rose Alice, and make his new life secure, he rides into town to confront the stranger who wants him dead.

ROB HILL

SHERIFF OF VENGEANCE

Complete and Unabridged

LINFORD
Leicester

First published in Great Britain in 2012 by
Robert Hale Limited
London

First Linford Edition
published 2013
by arrangement with
Robert Hale Limited
London

A catalogue record for this book is available
from the British Library.

ISBN 978–1–4448–1634–1

Published by
F. A. Thorpe (Publishing)
Anstey, Leicestershire

Set by Words & Graphics Ltd.
Anstey, Leicestershire
Printed and bound in Great Britain by
T. J. International Ltd., Padstow, Cornwall

This book is printed on acid-free paper

To Val and Joss

1

'There's a man in town who wants you dead.'

The rider looked down from his horse.

'Me?'

Clay Butterfield's shotgun shook in his hands.

'Sent me to find out where you live,' the rider said.

Clay stood in front of his cabin door.

'Now I know.'

The snow was luminous in the fading light. It clung to the branches of the tulip poplars, covered the fields and disguised the track from Vengeance along which the rider had found his way. Snow was heaped over the roof of the cabin and built odd shapes in the yard where it covered the log pile and the chicken coop. The men's breath made clouds of ice crystals in front of their faces. A line of smoke rose straight up from the cabin chimney. The cold held everything still and, apart from the rasp of the horse's breath, made everything quiet. Clay's shotgun pointed at the rider's chest.

'You're lyin',' Clay said.

Clay's eyes were piercing blue and patches of downy hair grew on his young cheeks. His hat was pulled down low against the cold and a scarf, a strip of old blanket, was wrapped around his neck. His jacket was repaired and threadbare and his leather boots were split along the seam. He handled the shotgun awkwardly.

'How old are you, mister?' the rider said.

'Don't matter,' Clay said. 'I'm the one with the scatter-gun, ain't I?'

The rider looked down at him with hard brown eyes. His weather-beaten face was marked with the pale line of a knife scar. He wore a black jacket and his hat carried a dusting of frost. His saddle was tooled with Mexican designs and the pommel was silver. He had a Winchester in a saddle holster and a canteen and a bedroll tied on behind.

Flakes of snow half the size of playing cards fell from a pewter sky.

'What's his name?'

'Eli Pitch.'

'Never heard of him,' Clay said. 'You rode out here to tell me this? I don't even know you.'

'That ain't all.'

The shotgun wavered in Clay's hands.

'Got a business proposition for you.'

The cabin door opened and a teenage girl, a little younger than Clay, stood there. She looked half starved. Her glassy skin was taut over her cheekbones and her eyes were bright. Her pale hair fell loosely and her fingers were white where she supported herself against the door frame. She wore a grey cotton house dress which was too big for her and a piece of linen embroidered with flowers hung over her shoulder.

'You talkin' to yourself, Clay?'

She jumped when she saw the rider. Her thumb went automatically to her mouth and she stared at him as though she was watching from the corner of a room. The rider touched his hat to her. She continued to watch him without acknowledgement.

'Get back inside, Rose Alice,' Clay said. 'You'll catch your death.'

The girl stared for a moment longer and then closed the door.

'Best put your horse in the barn and come on inside the house,' Clay said. 'My wife gets nervous.'

The rider noticed how Clay emphasized the words 'my wife' as if saying them was a novelty to him. Clay lowered the shotgun and watched the man dismount.

Night was closing on the farm. Shadows moved through the trees and invaded the yard. Clay led the way to the barn. It took a moment for their eyes to get used to the darkness. Horses stirred as they entered.

'We can talk later,' Clay said, 'when my wife's asleep.'

He fetched an armful of hay and set it down in front of the horse while the rider loosened the saddle. Clay watched as the man brushed his horse, patted her flank and whispered in her ear. He loosened a rolled blanket from the saddle and spread it over the horse's back.

'Obliged,' the rider said. He held out his hand to Clay. 'Zachariah York.'

'Clay Butterfield.' Clay shook the man's hand.

A screech owl's cry tore the silence and made the horses shift and stamp. Outside, the snow shone in the darkness. Orange firelight showed through the cracks in the shuttered cabin windows. The men's boots crunched over the frozen ground as they crossed the yard to the house.

A pillow of warm air which reeked of sweet stewing onions and the sourness of a chicken coop greeted the men as they entered the cabin. A skillet bubbled on an open fire in the stone chimney. The room was simply furnished. There was a table, two wooden chairs and a bed in the corner. A tallow candle in a carved wooden holder stood in the centre of the table waiting to be lit. An opened letter leaned against it. A goat was tethered to the end of the bed and chickens pecked at the floorboards.

Rose Alice had been standing beside the fire stirring the soup. She backed away as they entered, slipped her thumb into her mouth and watched the men.

'This here's Mr Zeke York,' Clay said. 'And this here's my wife, Rose Alice.'

Zeke propped his Winchester beside Clay's shotgun by the door. He took off his coat and hat. There were no pegs by the door but there was a horseshoe nailed up for luck. Zeke dropped his coat on the floor.

'Ma'am.' Zeke nodded a greeting.

Rose Alice stared.

'Mr York's rode out here on business,' Clay said.

'Coldest ride of my life,' Zeke said.

Clay moved a chair to the fireside and gestured to Zeke to sit. Rose Alice turned away from the men and ran a ladle through the thin soup.

Zeke let the warmth of the fire soak into him. He spread out his hands as if he were holding back the blaze then rubbed them together. Rose Alice watched him out of the corner of her eye. She put down the ladle and sat down on the edge of the bed, picked up the embroidered linen and placed it carefully over her shoulder so that it touched the pale skin of her neck. A hatchet was propped beside the bed.

'Most welcome fire I ever sat by,' Zeke said. 'Even if it does stink in here.'

He looked round the room until his eyes rested on a homemade fiddle with no strings which hung on a nail next to the chimney.

'You a musician?'

Zeke stretched his legs out to feel the heat on the inside of his calves. He noticed Rose Alice slip her thumb into her mouth and look away from him.

'Used to be,' Clay said.

He looked at Rose Alice.

'Second winter we've had up here,' Clay said. 'Worse last year. Snow started falling last week in October, didn't stop till March. This year it's been stop start all along. We thought the snow had finished, now we got a late fall.'

Rose Alice ladled soup into two tin mugs and set them on the table. She fetched pieces of hard tack, set them beside the mugs and went back to sit on the edge of the bed.

'I'm starved,' Clay said.

'Only two?' Zeke said.

'Looks like Rose Alice ain't hungry,' Clay explained. 'She don't hardly ever eat. Some days she won't touch a thing.'

Clay laughed nervously and dipped the hard tack into the soup.

Zeke looked at Rose Alice. Her thin face was a mask. She stared back at him, seeing and not seeing. She leaned her head so that the skin of her neck touched the embroidered cloth over her shoulder.

'So where're you from, mister?' Clay asked.

'Knoxville,' Zeke said. 'Went back after the war but didn't stay.'

'When I came back here after the war, there wasn't nothing left neither,' Clay said. 'My folks were dead, the house was all pulled down. There's two other farms in this valley. Johnny Rebs picked on this place and left the others alone. My uncle had a place south of Frankfort. There wasn't nothing left there neither. I found Rose Alice livin' in the barn.'

Rose Alice stared into the fire, the soft skin of her neck nestled against the embroidered flowers.

'She was livin' at your uncle's place?' Zeke said.

'We're cousins.' Clay laughed. 'Pretty much growed up together. Paid a dollar for a wedding licence and got married first time a travellin' preacher came through.'

Firelight flickered over the younger man's face. Zeke saw a mixture of pride and disappointment written there; pride because he was describing his place in the world; disappointment because of the way things had worked out. Clay leaned towards him and lowered his voice, anxious to explain how hard times had been.

'Sold off the timber from my uncle's house to a neighbour. Couldn't get nothin' for the land. We moved back here an' repaired the house. Bought some hogs and a calf.'

Clay took a leather pouch from his pocket and shook some tobacco into the palm of his hand. He rolled a cigarette and touched the end against a log in the fire to light it. Rose Alice lay down on the bed facing the wall and drew her legs up beside her. Thinking she was asleep, Clay got up and covered his wife with a blanket but her eyes were open.

'What happened?' Zeke said.

Clay stared at the floor.

'Winter came. Hogs died,' he said. 'Calf got took by wolves.'

'Wolves this far south?' Zeke said.

'Come down from the mountains when the weather's bad. They've been troublin' us this year too.'

A log tumbled out of the fire in a burst of sparks. Clay kicked it back in place and put another on top. Rose Alice lay still. Clay leaned over to see if she was asleep but she was staring at the wall.

'So whatever it is you're sellin', we can't afford to buy it,' Clay said. 'Anyhow, we ain't stayin' round here. Wagon train leaves for California next week. We got a wagon.'

'Next week?' Zeke said.

'Soon as the snow's gone. Plan to start out while the ground's hard. Be crossin' the Rockies in the fall.'

'How much money have you got?' Zeke said.

Clay looked sharply at him.

'It's all right,' Zeke said. 'I was just askin'.'

'A hundred dollars,' Clay said. 'In the bank, in town. We was hopin' the mining company would buy the farm but they turned us down. Said they would reconsider if they could buy land further on down the valley at the same time. No one else wants to sell.'

Clay looked over at Rose Alice. Her back was turned and she lay still. He took a last draw on his cigarette and flicked the end into the fire.

'Must be good huntin' around here,' Zeke said. 'Deer an' winter hares and such. I mean you don't need store bought coffee to survive.'

Clay stared morosely into the flames.

Rose Alice sat bolt upright as if she'd been burned. She stared at the two men.

'He can't shoot straight. He goes out huntin' all day an' he don't bring nothin' back. That's the truth.'

She swung her thin legs over the side of the bed, quickly brushed her dress down over them and stood up.

'You see how we gotta live?' she said to Zeke. 'Sometimes I forget whether animals are living in the house with us or we're living in a pen with them.'

Firelight flickered over the bones of her face and her eyes shone.

'I got a screw o' coffee in my saddle-bag, ma'am. Why don't you put that on to boil for us?'

Rose Alice giggled. 'Real coffee?'

'Ma'am.'

'My husband says he don't like real coffee,' she said. 'He only likes acorn. That's why we ain't got no real coffee.'

'Rose Alice . . . ' Clay began. 'Please.'

'Just like he can't bring home nothin' when he goes huntin' and we have to live on onion soup all winter,' she continued. 'Just like he sold my daddy's house where it was warm an' we had to come an' live here in this cold place. Just like he let the hogs die an' the calf die.'

'We're going to California where it's warm all the time,' Clay said. 'You just

13

keep thinking of that.'

Rose Alice put her thumb in her mouth and wrapped the linen round her neck like a scarf.

'You should try an' eat, even if it is just onion soup.'

Clay stood and ladled a cupful of soup from the skillet and held it out to her. She took her thumb out of her mouth and leaned forward, a faint smile playing over her lips. Instead of taking the cup she swiped it away, splashing the soup over Zeke and sending the tin cup clattering across the floor. Shocked, Zeke recoiled backwards, stumbling against the table and knocking over his chair. Instinct made his hand fly to his gun. Clay grabbed his arm. But there was no need, he had recovered himself. Rose Alice put her thumb back into her mouth and stared into the fire.

'Damn me.' Zeke wiped his face. 'She's like a spoilt kid. How old is she?'

'She ain't well,' Clay said. 'She ain't been well since the war.'

Rose Alice took her thumb out of her

mouth. Her eyes bored into Zeke.

'I'm sixteen and a married woman. This is my house. If I say I don't want no soup, I don't want no soup.'

She lay down again, faced the wall and drew her knees up beside her.

Clay crossed over to the bed. He smoothed the top of her head lightly and lifted the blanket over her shoulders.

'Hush now,' he said. 'I'll go out in the mornin' an' bring back a rabbit. I promise.'

He reached down and stacked another log on the fire. The wood crackled and the flames danced. Then he sat beside her on the edge of the bed and rested his hand on her shoulder. He stayed there for a while, staring into the fire, waiting to feel her relax. Zeke found a whiskey bottle in his saddlebag and took a slug. He left the bottle on the table for Clay.

When Rose Alice was asleep, Clay returned to the table.

'She'll be fine in the mornin'.'

Zeke pushed the whiskey bottle over to Clay. He wiped the top on his sleeve and took a mouthful. The red-eye burned his throat and left him coughing for breath.

'She really sixteen?' Zeke said.

'Fourteen when I married her.'

'So what does that make you?'

'Seventeen.'

'Means you was kinda young to be in the army, never mind marrying your cousin.'

'Wasn't no choice,' Clay said.

'Which regiment?'

'Ain't one for talking about the war,' Clay said. 'One side won, but everyone lost from what I seen. Best forget about it now.'

Zeke took another pull from the bottle.

'Anyhow,' Clay went on, 'now you can tell me why you come out here. Just keep your voice low.'

Zeke looked across the table at him. The scar on his cheek was livid in the firelight. He ran his fingers through his grey hair. His lined face evidenced years on the trail.

'Got a proposition for you,' he began.

Zeke's brown eyes held Clay's gaze.

'I got a way of keeping you alive.'

Clay pushed his chair back and laughed.

'Mister, I've been working on that one, I can tell you.'

Zeke glanced over at the bed. Rose Alice was lying still. He lowered his voice to a whisper and spoke quickly. Clay leaned across the table to catch his words.

'Like I said when I first got here, there's a fella in town wants to kill you. I rode with him in the war. Only a matter of time before he finds his way out here.'

'Why should he want to kill me?'

Clay glanced round at Rose Alice. She lay still with her back to the men.

'In the war, his farm was burned. Everything he owned was took. Believes his family was killed. He said he knows the names of all the fellas in the squad that done it.'

Zeke paused and leaned over the table towards Clay.

'You're next on his list.'

Clay's voice caught in his throat.

'That can't be.'

Zeke smiled.

'Your unit down in Knoxville during the war?'

'Sure.'

'Go in for any barn burning?'

'Everyone did. Both sides.'

'He's a deliberate man. I wouldn't have rode out here if I thought he was foolin'.'

'You've come to tell me this?'

'I said I rode out with a proposition.'

Clay tried to read the stranger's face.

'You pay me and I'll kill him for you.'

2

It was early afternoon and the saloon was empty. The door was shut tight against the cold and condensation misted the windows. A wood stove in the corner punched out the heat which filled most of the room. Tom Farrow, saloon owner, barkeep and town mayor was working his way through rows of glasses with a cotton cloth and lining them up with a perfectionist's eye. Farrow was dressed for business. He wore a white apron which reached the ground and a clean collarless shirt with the sleeves rolled up. He was close shaven, pale and his hair was centre parted.

Farrow was proud of his saloon: the place was clean and the drinks were hardly watered at all. He was proud of his town: the post-war rebuilding meant good wages and since hostilities ended, business had revived. But this winter there had been visits from the Regulators, night riders who raged against the outcome of the war and who had acquired a taste for the violence they experienced on the killing fields. They sought out trouble and a sleepy Kentucky farm town was easy pickings. Tom Farrow was sure of one thing: Vengeance needed a new sheriff.

A girl went from table to table polishing each one to a dull shine, aware that Farrow was watching and knowing that if he was not completely satisfied he would make her do them all again. This was Nicolette. She had come up from Louisiana with her husband, Pierre, late in the fall intending to join a wagon train bound for California. They had arrived just as the first snow fell and had no option but to wait out the winter. Pierre was a good carpenter and picked up repair work around town while Nicolette cleaned at the saloon and the store. They lived in their wagon which was parked up in the lee of the livery stables at the end of the street.

After she finished the last table, Nicolette looked at Farrow who nodded approval. She gathered her brush, pan and the polishing cloths and went upstairs to continue her work there. She had expected to see her husband who often came in for a hand of cards in the middle of the day. He was late. He had told her he would finish the roof he was working on by lunchtime.

Eli Pitch was the only customer in the saloon. He had arrived in town with another man before the latest snowfall a few days previously. He sat at the table nearest the stove with a whiskey at hand. He riffled a pack of cards, dealt Euchre hands to imaginary players, swept up the cards and dealt again. Tom Farrow noted the ease with which he handled the cards, the expensive black leather gunbelt at his hip and the two fingers missing from his left hand. The men who used the saloon were store keepers, farmers and surveyors from the Cumberland Mining Company passing through. Pitch was unlike any of them. But he had paid in advance for a room and played cards with anyone who cared to join him. No one knew why he was in town and so far no one had cared to ask.

The door burst open and Pierre stood there with snow in his hair. He headed straight for the stove and held his hands out flat above it, palms down.

'Nicolette?' he said.

'Upstairs,' Farrow said. 'Just finished in here.'

Pierre nodded.

'Cold as hell on that roof.'

Pitch shuffled the deck and began to lay out another hand.

'You lookin' for a game, mister?' Pierre said.

'Why not?' Pitch said, without looking up.

Pierre sat down. He saw Eli Pitch properly now. He took in his weather-beaten face, saw how fast he dealt the cards and realized straight away he was out of his league.

'Shouldn't we wait and see if anyone else comes in?' Pierre said.

Pitch shrugged.

'Sheriff should be along,' Farrow said. 'He don't ever say no to a hand of Euchre.'

Pierre brightened.

'Let's wait for the sheriff.'

Pitch dealt another hand, swept in the cards and dealt again. Pierre studied him. Was he dealing from the bottom of the deck? Pierre couldn't be sure. Pitch's lack of conversation made him edgy.

'You ain't been in town long,' Pierre said.

Pitch shuffled the cards and started to deal.

'Me and my wife stayed the winter,' Pierre went on. 'Headin' out to California the minute the thaw comes.'

Eli swept up the cards.

'Got a wagon all kitted out by the stable.'

Pierre realized he was the only one

23

talking and fell silent. The glasses chinked as Farrow lined them up behind the bar. Pitch snapped the cards as he concentrated on another shuffle.

The door opened. Farrow and Pierre looked towards it. Sheriff Jim Parsons stepped over to the bar.

'Gimme one of your warm-me-ups, Tommy.'

With a single, deft movement Farrow filled a whiskey glass until the meniscus hovered above the brim.

Sheriff Parsons was a cheerful, round-faced man with twinkling eyes and a nicotine moustache which drooped over his mouth. He was the proprietor of Parsons' Hardware across the street and had taken on the role of honorary sheriff as a matter of civic duty. A tin star gleamed on the lapel of his jacket and he wore a pair of Colts, although he had never fired a shot in anger.

He downed the whiskey in one.

'You boys playin' gin?'

'No,' Pitch said. 'Heard you was

comin' by an' might like a game of Cutthroat.'

Parsons sat down.

'That's mighty nice. Ain't nothin' better than a three handed game. Some folks are partial to four handed Euchre but not me.'

He nodded a greeting to Pierre and turned to Pitch.

'Don't believe I know you, mister. I'm Sheriff Parsons.'

'Eli Pitch.'

'Passin' through or plannin' on stayin'?'

'Stayin',' Pitch said.

He riffled the cards and dealt five each. The men studied their hands.

'Four tricks a point,' Pitch said. 'Five for a march. We playin' for money?'

'I . . . ' Pierre began.

'Don't matter,' Pitch said.

Parsons called up trumps and the game began.

Farrow watched for a while, left the whiskey bottle on the bar for the sheriff's refill and headed upstairs to check Nicolette's cleaning.

'So what brings you to this part of the county?' Parsons said. 'I know Pierre here is heading out any day now.'

'Two things. I'm a negotiator for Cumberland Mining and I came lookin' for people from the war,' Eli said. 'They was down around Knoxville, Campbell's Station.'

Parsons laughed.

'Most fellas round here was at Knoxville. I was with the 23rd right the way through. Who were you with?'

'Come from there,' Pitch said. 'Had a farm off the Concord Road, just a mile from Campbell's.'

Parsons put his cards down.

'I never went there. Never heard of it. Just rode into Knoxville. Never fired a shot.'

'Clay Butterfield,' Pitch said. 'He knows the place.'

'Clay?' Parsons said. 'He was our bugler. Wasn't old enough to have been in the army at all.'

Parsons laughed.

'We talkin' or playin'?' Pierre said.

'Playin',' Parsons said. 'Whose turn is it?'

'Mine,' Pitch said.

'No it ain't,' Parsons said.

Pitch rounded on him. Rage twisted his face but his words were cold and purposeful.

'I said it's my turn. When you blue bellies came through on your ride to Knoxville, you took everything I had. Everything. Killed my family, looted my house, burned my farm.'

'Mister . . . ' Parsons protested.

'Set fire to it all,' Pitch said. 'So don't you go sayin' you never fired a shot.'

Parsons' chair scraped on the wooden floor as he stood up. His face was mottled and his voice shook.

'Stop this now. War's over. All the records are destroyed. Ain't nobody kin tell who did what.'

'I know who did it,' Pitch said. 'I got the names of everyone in that unit. Your name is right there amongst them.'

'You come here for recompense? Is

that what you're sayin'? You want us to repay you for what you lost?'

'Too late for that now,' Eli said.

Parsons seemed at a loss.

'Then what have you come for?'

In a second, Pitch measured up the sheriff with a gun-fighter's eye, took in his height, weight, the way he held himself and knew he could outdraw him.

'Vengeance,' Pitch said gently.

For a moment, the word hung in the air between them.

'What?'

'I'm gonna kill you an' I'm gonna take what's yours.'

Parsons went for his gun. But his hand was slow. A shot split the afternoon air and then he was staring down in disbelief at the red stain which spread across his chest before he could draw. He looked up at Pitch for a second. Bewilderment masked his face. He toppled backwards, bringing down the table and scattering the cards.

Horrified, Pierre backed away towards

the door. Pitch reached down, pulled Parsons' Colt from its holster and shot Pierre in the chest. The force of the shot kicked him backwards over the tables. There was shouting upstairs and the sound of running feet. Pitch stepped over to Pierre, pressed the sheriff's gun into his hand and folded his index finger round the trigger. He took a handful of coins and dollar bills from his own pocket and flung them over the floor.

Footsteps clattered on the stairs. There was shouting and a woman's scream. Then Nicolette barged Pitch aside and threw herself down beside Pierre. She cradled his head in her arms, talking to him softly, her words spilling over his face. She told him to wake up, that she was there, that everything would be all right. Her tears splashed over him and mixed with the blood on his shirt. She began to moan, a low unearthly sound which came from somewhere deep within her. Tom Farrow rested his hand on her shoulder, but she shook him off. She didn't look up, but kept her gaze fastened on Pierre. She touched the patch of blood which covered the front of his shirt and peered at the red stain on her finger tips, barely able to believe what she saw. She smoothed Pierre's hair away from his forehead, leaned forward and kissed him.

Farrow stepped away from Pitch.

'Why d'you do it, mister?'

Pitch holstered his gun.

'One minute we were playin', next he was callin' the sheriff all kinds o' names,' Pitch explained. 'Called him a cheatin' sonofabitch. Said he'd stolen his money.'

'Pierre said this?' Farrow said. His voice was faint. He gripped the back of a chair to steady himself.

'Made a dive for the sheriff's gun and shot 'im. Next thing, he swung on me. What could I do?'

'You weren't playing for money,' Farrow said. 'I heard you ask 'em.'

He caught sight of the banknotes and

coins scattered across the floor and his voice faded. He leaned down and ran his hand over Sheriff Parsons' face to close his eyes.

'Young fella insisted on it,' Pitch said. 'Reckoned he could make a buck, I guess.'

'I never knowed Pierre play for money,' Farrow said.

People were at the door now. Shocked faces.

'This man shot Sheriff Jim Parsons over cards,' Pitch announced. His voice was calm and carried the force of authority. 'I killed him to stop him shooting me. Parsons was too slow. This man was able to snatch his gun and shoot him with it. You had the wrong man as sheriff.'

Each member of the crowd was stooped as if a great weight pressed on him. They listened to Pitch in shocked silence.

'What do you say happened, Tommy?' someone called.

'I was upstairs,' Farrow said. 'I left the sheriff's whiskey on the bar and went upstairs.'

'I seen hot heads before,' Pitch said. 'People passin' through a town. This fella was a Cajun wasn't he? You got to have a strong sheriff.'

'Jim Parsons was sheriff because no one else would do it,' Farrow continued. 'This is a small place. No one here makes trouble.'

'You get people passin' through?' Pitch asked. 'Wagons on their way to the territories? Regulators ridin' through at night?'

The people in the crowd nodded and voices called out in agreement. There was danger and they hadn't realized it until now. Farrow leaned over Nicolette again to try to offer her some comfort. She shoved him away.

'You're lyin', mister,' Nicolette screamed. 'Pierre never hurt no one in his life.'

She flung herself at Pitch and swung punches at his face. Her fist caught his jaw and blood burst from his lip. Pitch held her off. Farrow grabbed her, pulled her away and held her close. Daggers of anger flashed in Pitch's eyes.

'I told you what happened,' Pitch snarled. 'The evidence is right here.'

He pointed to the money scattered across the floor and the gun in her dead husband's hand.

3

Wolves circled the cabin. Woken by their scratching at the door, Clay stood by the window and watched them slip across the moonlit yard. When they left the cabin, they headed for the stable, surrounded it, sniffed at the bottom of the door and clawed wherever there was the smallest gap in the wooden walls. Unable to find a way in, they returned to the cabin to try again there.

Rose Alice joined Clay at the window. She pulled an old grey blanket round herself with one hand and grasped a hatchet in the other.

'Same dream?' Clay said.

'Always the same,' she said. 'You know that.'

The wolf pack fanned out across the yard. They caught the scent of the chicken coop and pawed away the snow.

'End in the same way?'

'I killed him.' Rose Alice sounded bored. 'Like always.'

The wolves broke open the henhouse door and scrabbled inside, their frenzy building. A minute later they emerged disappointed and streaked over to try the barn again.

'How long's he stayin'?' Rose Alice said.

She nodded at Zeke who lay asleep on his bedroll in front of the dying fire, the drained whiskey bottle beside him.

'It ain't snowed no more, so he'll leave in the morning.'

A lump of snow crashed down from the branches of one of the tulip poplars. The wolves scattered out of the yard.

'We'll build the fire when it's light,' Clay said.

He put his arm round Rose Alice's shoulder and gently took the hatchet from her hand.

'Lay it down by the bed,' she said.

Clay closed the shutter.

★ ★ ★

A gunshot woke Zeke. Outside somewhere. Not close. He sat up. The cabin was freezing, the goat was chewing his bedroll and the place stank. The same unlit tallow candle was on the table with the letter beside it. Apart from the chickens and the goat, he was on his own. Gagging for fresh air, Zeke kept the goat at bay with his foot, rolled up his blanket, pulled on his boots and flung open the cabin door. Melting icicles dripped from the broken porch rail and a block of snow slid off the cabin roof. He noticed how animals had broken into the chicken coop in the night. Two sets of footprints ploughed from the cabin door to the field beyond the trees. Another shot echoed.

Back inside, Zeke pulled on his coat and trod round the chicken droppings which carpeted the floor. He set to work lighting the fire from the heap of kindling on the hearth. He shaved pieces of bark and twig into a pile with his Bowie and made a spark with his flint. When a wood shaving glowed red he blew on it softly until a flame popped. He heaped on more wood shavings and twigs and watched as the flames bit and a breeze drew the fire up the chimney. Zeke decided that even if he had to put up with the chickens, the stinking goat could stay outside for a while. The animal bared its teeth at him as he hauled it out on to the porch and tied it to the rail.

As a grey squirrel leaped through the high branches of the tulip poplars, Zeke caught sight of Clay and Rose Alice through the trees. Rose Alice held the shotgun up to her shoulder while Clay stood behind her with his arms round hers supporting the gun. A shooting lesson. Clay held her close, his head next to hers. As they squinted along the barrel together, they were laughing.

Lead clouds covered the sky. Nothing moved apart from the occasional crash of snow falling from the high branches. Zeke's breath hung in front of his face and he shivered as the cold cut through his coat. He heard the thud of the shotgun again and Rose Alice's laughter jingle over the frozen land. The goat snarled at him as he stepped inside the cabin and shut the door.

The fire had taken and Zeke encouraged the blaze with kindling from the pile beside the grate. The wood crackled and spat but warmth had not yet spread out into the room. Hunger gnawed his belly. There was hard tack in his saddlebag and watery onion soup left in the pan from last night. He settled down to wait by the fire in the hope that Clay would come back with a rabbit.

Later, Zeke heard Clay and Rose Alice stamping the snow off their boots on the porch. The door burst open and they tumbled inside, their cheeks scoured by the cold. Rose Alice was towing the goat after her. Clay stood the shotgun by the door.

'Why d'you tether him out on the porch?' Rose Alice looked Zeke in the eye. 'D'you want him to freeze to death?'

'Never mind that,' Clay interrupted. 'You gonna tend to that sourdough, like you said, Rose Alice?'

'We've only got one goat,' Rose Alice continued. 'An' we aim to take him to California with us. That's why we keep him in here, in the warm. Any fool can see that. Why d'you build up a fire an' tie him up outside?'

She picked up the piece of embroidered linen and draped it round her shoulders like a shawl.

'Didn't shoot nothin'?' Zeke asked.

'Only saw one hare,' Clay said. 'He was too fast for us. Winged him though. There was blood on the snow.'

Rose Alice moved the candlestick and the letter from the table and set down the bowl of sourdough and a crock of flour. She pushed up the sleeves of her dress and became absorbed in her work.

'There's squirrels out there,' Clay said. 'I seen 'em.'

He stood up, buckled on his gunbelt and stepped out on to the porch. He left the door open so they could see him take aim. He held his Colt high, steadied the gun on his forearm and squinted along the sight. At the first shot, a squirrel tumbled out of the trees. Clay fetched it and dropped it on the table.

'Took his head clean off,' he said.

Rose Alice pulled the linen close round her neck.

'Maybe we should check on the horses while Rose Alice cooks up a stew,' Clay said.

The edge of the barn door was clawed and splintered. Teeth marks scarred the wood. The wolves had been close to breaking in.

'Bite through a wall if they're hungry enough,' Zeke said. 'You'll need to strengthen this before nightfall.'

Inside the barn, most of the space was taken up by a wagon. It was old but the wheels looked sound and the sides had been repaired with clumsy carpentry. The canvas roof was down and piled untidily beside it.

'I thought about what you said,' Clay said. 'You ain't told me how much.'

A rat skittered through the straw. Clay took a shovel and broke the ice on the water trough.

'You told me you got a hundred dollars,' Zeke said. 'So that's the price.'

Clay rested the shovel against a pillar. He started to kick the loose straw into a pile.

'Barn needs sweepin',' he said.

'That and the deeds to the farm.'

Clay looked at him.

'That's all we got.'

'Hundred dollars an' the deeds to a place you can't sell don't seem so much in exchange for stayin' alive.'

'I'll go into town and talk to this Eli Pitch,' Clay said.

'You take one step inside a room that he's in, you're a dead man,' Zeke said.

'I'll shoot him then.'

'Mister, you can't hit a rabbit with a scattergun. How are you gonna face down a gunfighter in a saloon?'

Clay found a yard broom by the door

41

and started to sweep up the loose straw.

'I ain't about to part with no hundred dollars. That's the seed corn for our new life.'

The strokes of Clay's broom raised dust from the dry earth floor. The horses moved in their stalls.

'There's another way,' Zeke said.

Clay carried on working. Dust sparkled in the lines of grey light which entered through the gaps in the walls.

'I'll take your wife as a trade.'

Clay stopped sweeping and turned to him.

'I should shoot you for that.'

Zeke shrugged.

'Just a business proposition. I don't mean nothing by it.'

'You can get outta here right now.'

'She's weak,' Zeke said. 'She ain't gonna make it to California. Do you know how many graves there are out there on the prairies?'

'She's sick,' Clay said. 'She'll get better.'

'She needs a life in a town, not being

dragged two thousand miles in an old wagon.'

'You just saddle up and get outa here,' Clay said.

'You think about what I said,' Zeke said. 'About the money and the deeds. Just let me have something to eat before I go.'

'I ain't giving you nothing.'

Zeke heaved his saddle up on to his horse while Clay went back to the cabin to fetch the rifle for him. He returned with the Winchester and a handful of hard tack in one hand and his shotgun in the other.

Pale sunlight pushed through the cloud and melting snow dripped from the barn roof as Zeke rode out. Clay stood by the cabin door and watched him.

'You're a dead man,' Zeke called as he passed the cabin. 'I could have saved you and you turned me down.'

As soon as Zeke was some distance down the track, Clay went back inside. Rose Alice was feeding squirrel bones to the chickens.

'I'm gonna ride out to Bill Choke's place,' Clay said. 'How long's that stew gonna be?'

'What for?'

'There's some fella in town got a grudge against our old unit. I gotta warn Bill. Might ride on to John Anderson's after that.'

Rose Alice glanced over at the hatchet which was propped against the side of the bed. She tightened the embroidered linen round her throat.

'Half an hour before the stew's ready. If that fella's gone, I'll put a potato in it.'

'If I leave in half an hour, I'll be back by dark.'

Clay went out to the barn and saddled his horse. He ran his hand over the shafts of the wagon. Just a few days, he thought. A week at the outside. They'd join up with Pierre and Nicolette and other wagons would come up from the south. It had been his idea to start out as soon as the thaw came. The nights would be cold but the going would be good over the hard ground. And they were ready. All they needed was a day to go into town to buy supplies and half a day to load the wagon. The only job which remained was to make cages for the chickens.

Bill Choke's farm lay two miles round the shoulder of the valley and John Anderson's place was two beyond that. If the three of them went into town together, they could see off this gunslinger, whoever he was. Clay had known Bill and John all his life. Being a few years younger than them, they had been his boyhood heroes. They had shown him all the creeks and gullies in the mountains beyond the valley and taken him on summer expeditions up to the high ridges. When the war came, they joined the 23rd together and managed to get posted to the same unit. Clay lied about his age to join them. They were strong men who battled the freezing winters and blazing summers in order to survive in this unforgiving land. They would not let him down.

'Leave the scattergun,' Rose Alice said.

She wore the embroidered linen tight around her neck and slipped her thumb into her mouth as she watched Clay eat.

'This stew's good,' Clay said. 'You should try some yourself.'

Clay looked at her and she met his gaze. To him, her pale eyes, sharp cheek bones and corn coloured hair made her seem fragile and beautiful.

'You wearin' your rabbit's foot?'

'I left it somewhere,' Clay said.

'I'll find it.' Rose Alice stood up. 'I don't want you riding without it.'

4

'Can't help you, Clay.'

Clay had found Bill Choke out shooting quail on the eastern edge of his land. As he rode through Choke's farm, he noticed how the fences were all in good repair and the gates hung on new hinges.

Choke frowned. He was a powerfully built, square-shouldered man. He was a good shot, hard working, cautious and modest. He thought of himself as generous, always ready to help a neighbour. But this was different. The war had been hell. He had seen atrocities and found that he was capable of doing things which meant he was scarcely able to recognize himself. Since he left the army, he had buried himself in his farm work, tried to forget the fighting and taken little notice of what went on in the outside world.

He'd heard about men who still carried the war with them and wished to have nothing to do with them. He shook his head.

'Knoxville?'

Choke's dog, Otto, a tousled mongrel, lay obediently at his feet.

He vaguely remembered a row of burning buildings along the road which led to the town. How they came to be on fire, he couldn't say. It could have been his unit or some other. He had seen burning houses every day and had torched some of them himself, though two years on he couldn't remember where or even how many times he had done this. The only thing he remembered about Knoxville was that it had been undefended: the 23rd had ridden into town without firing a shot.

'He's got a list of the names in our unit,' Clay said.

'You believe that?' Choke said. 'There ain't no lists. Everything was destroyed.'

As he spoke, he remembered the

French mantelpiece clock he had brought home after one of the campaigns as a present for his wife. He had found it in some plantation house but because he had seen so many ransacked houses, he couldn't say exactly where it had been.

'Said I was next,' Clay said.

Bill Choke heard fear echo in Clay's voice. He remembered Clay as a kid, always tagging along after him and John Anderson on their fishing trips, always wanting them to show him how to set traps, always struggling to keep up when they went on expeditions up into the mountains. He remembered what a poor shot Clay was and how he and John had laughed at him.

Choke laughed now.

'Can't be,' he said.

'I thought if the three of us, you, John and me rode into town . . . '

'Said I can't help you, Clay.'

'He could come looking for you,' Clay said.

'Anyone sets foot on my farm, I'll

shoot him,' Choke said. 'But I ain't going into town in search of trouble.'

Choke raised his shotgun, squinted along the sights and squeezed the trigger. The sound of the shot rolled around the valley and a quail lay in a splash of its blood on the snow. He gave the command and Otto sprang after the fallen bird.

Clay turned his horse in the direction of Anderson's place further down the valley. He pulled his jacket tight around him and urged the horse on. He had not expected Bill to let him down. Disappointment weighed heavily on him.

Patches of grass showed through the thawing snow and water dripped from the tree branches as Clay skirted the forest edge. A grey fox watched him pass and a pair of goldfinches darted between the branches like flame. Pale sunlight brightened the transparent sky. After a mile, Clay could see the smoke from the Andersons' farmhouse chimney rising over the brow of the hill.

Clay feared John Anderson's reaction now. Would it be the same as Choke's? The men had always been close. They had always prized loyalty and friendship above all else, but the war had made Bill want to look after his own. Could Clay blame him for that? Clay was certain of one thing. If the tables had been turned and Bill had asked him for help, he wouldn't have hesitated. He knew it.

Being further away from the town, both Choke's and Anderson's farms had escaped destruction in the war. The Confederate regiment which rode through had missed the eastern end of the valley. When the men returned, they were able to take up farming where they had left off, unlike Clay who had had to begin by rebuilding his house. When he announced that he and Rose Alice were going to quit Kentucky and head west, he had expected Choke or Anderson, as his closest neighbours, to make an offer for his land. It puzzled him that neither had. They were not prosperous yet, but they worked hard and in a few years they would be. Either of them could have afforded the interest on a loan.

The brow of the hill gave Clay a view of John Anderson's farm. The smoke which Clay had assumed was from the chimney, rose from the burned out ruin of the house. The blackened and charred roof beams stuck up at accusing angles out of the mess of charcoaled timber, shingle and the ashes of what had once been a home.

Clay rushed his horse down the hillside. As he got nearer, the bitter smell of burning filled his lungs. When he reached the smoking rubble, he leapt out of the saddle shouting John's name. He ran round the ruins, desperate to see some sign of life and dashed in amongst the ashes where the parlor had been. The heat seared the soles of his boots. He stopped and listened, straining to catch a reply, but there was just the wind moaning through a hackberry tree and the soft crash as thawing snow fell from its branches, nothing else.

Clay steadied himself and forced himself to take account of what he was seeing. The stink of burnt wood made it difficult to breathe. Where was everybody? He looked for cart tracks, for the marks of horses' hoofs, but the fire had melted the snow for yards around the house. Where were the horses? There had been a corral in front of the house but the fencing was trampled down and some of the fence posts had been pulled out of the ground. The gate swung open on broken hinges.

On the other side of the corral, the ruins of the barn smoldered. Like the house, there were a few blackened beams left but the walls and the roof were gone. Clay called out John's name again and again. Hurrying round the perimeter of where the barn had stood, peering into the piles of smoking ash and charred timber, Clay braced himself for the sight of the burned bodies of John Anderson and his family.

Clay's horse had begun to wander

away from the ruined buildings towards the treeline. He assumed that the stench of burning was too much for the animal. He was surprised to see her stop abruptly and look back as if she was expecting him to follow. Then he saw why. His boots slipped in the snow as he started to run. John's name caught in his throat as he started to call out again. The horse stood still and waited for Clay. The body of John's wife, Ellen, lay at the animal's feet; John's body was a few yards further on, face down in the snow. They had been shot in the back.

A great wave of fear shook Clay. He stumbled from one body to the other to check for signs of life, but the corpses were stiff and cold. Their eyes were open, their hair was crusted with frost and their skin was bleached. He scanned the treeline but there was no one. He checked the valley to the east but it was empty. High above, a lone black vulture circled, riding the thermals on its flat wings, the white feathered tips spread out like fingers.

Then something else caught Clay's eye. A few yards further on where the snow was disturbed by scrambled hoof prints, a black metal box lay open and upside down. Clay recognized it at once. All the farmers had one; there was one back at his cabin under the bed. The farmers kept the deeds to their property in it and whenever they needed a mortgage, deposited this box with the farm deeds in it at the bank. John Anderson's box was empty.

Clay knew a black vulture could kill and gut a pig, but the ground was too hard for him to bury the bodies. He salvaged timber and stones from the house to cover them where they lay — it would protect them for a while. The afternoon light had deepened before he finished.

Mounted up and with dusk gathering, Clay returned the way he had come. As he descended the hill on to Bill Choke's land, he paused to roll a cigarette while he considered riding up to the house to let him know. This would mean a two mile detour and darkness was close. What would be gained? Choke was ready to fight. You're next on his list, Zeke had said. Clay had to get home. Wolves were keeping pace with him behind the trees.

Moonlight lit the cabin and the tulip poplars. Snow had slipped from the roof while he had been away and patches of snow had melted in the yard. But there was no firelight visible through the cracks in the shutters. There was no light in the cabin at all. Why had Rose Alice let the fire die? Clay called out to let her know he was home like he always did so as not to startle her. No answer. Was she sleeping? He called again. Even though the night air had frozen him to the bone, he felt a bead of sweat form on the nape of his neck and trickle down his back. He called a third time.

A shot fractured the silence. A scattergun. Someone was shooting from the barn. Rose Alice was scared, that's all it was. She was scared so she had hidden in the barn and now he had surprised her.

'It's all right,' Clay shouted.

There was another shot then. A pistol. Away to the left, amongst the poplars. Clay heard the bullet sing through the night air. He backed his horse into the trees and slipped out of the saddle.

'Clay, that you?'

It was Rose Alice's voice, shrill with fear.

Another pistol shot cracked. The bullet bit a side of the barn this time.

'He means to kill me, Clay,' Rose Alice screamed.

There was a third pistol shot. A horse whinnied and stamped its feet in the shadows beneath the trees.

The shotgun fired again. Then the pistol once more. Clay heard a horse turn then hoof beats thud away over the hard ground. In the moonlight, he saw a rider low in the saddle gallop in the direction of the road.

'You scared him off,' Clay shouted.

In the barn, Clay had to prize the shotgun out of Rose Alice's grasp. Terror had locked her hands. She peered out into the darkness.

'You sure he's gone?'

Clay pulled off his jacket and slipped it over Rose Alice's shoulders. In the cabin, he drew up a chair for her and built the fire. The orange light flickered over the bones of her face as she stared into the flames. She reached over to the bed and found the strip of embroidered linen and slipped it round her neck.

'It was that man who was here before,' Rose Alice said. 'He said there's a man in Vengeance who aims to kill you, Clay. He said he wanted to take me away so this man wouldn't kill me too, but I wouldn't go.'

'You did well,' Clay said. 'I'm proud of you, Rose Alice.'

He knelt beside her, put his arm round her shoulder and drew her to him.

'Bill and John will help us, won't they Clay?'

The fire crackled. Rose Alice stared into it, watching the faces which came and went in the flames.

'We got anything to eat?' Clay said.

He found the skillet which contained the remains of the squirrel stew and set it to warm over the fire.

'It ain't ever cold in California,' Clay said. 'You only need a fire for cookin' on, even in winter. You just keep thinking on that.'

Clay stirred the soup and tasted a spoonful. He held the next spoonful up to Rose Alice's lips and she took it. He carried on like this, offering her alternate spoonfuls with him. Eventually she put her thumb in her mouth and shook her head when he held out the spoon again. Almost at once, she pushed him away and tried to get up.

'I ain't feelin' good,' she said. 'I can't keep nothin' down.'

Clay held her.

'You just try,' he said. 'I don't want

you goin' out back an' bein' sick tonight. You just sit still an' quiet with me.'

Rose Alice stopped struggling and held the linen shawl close round her neck.

'We got trouble comin',' Clay said. 'We got to be smart, Rose Alice. Both of us.'

He looked at her to make sure she was listening. He told her about Bill Choke and what had happened to the Andersons. He told her about John Anderson's empty deed box and the price Zeke had asked for helping them stay alive. Rose Alice stared into the dancing flames. Clay shoved another log on the fire and a fist of sparks burst into the room.

'Only one thing we can do,' Clay said. 'We gotta leave tonight.'

Rose Alice looked at him.

'I can load the wagon and harness the horses right now. Won't take more than a couple of hours. We can be away before first light. The ground is hard so we can cut right across country. We'll circle around the town and no one will see us.'

As Clay heard his own words, he began to believe in what he was saying. His plan was stronger when he spoke it aloud than it had been when it was just an idea in his head.

'We can keep right on goin',' he said. 'Pierre will hear soon enough. He'll know we've gone on ahead. He could catch us up in a week, two at the outside.'

Clay imagined Pierre and Nicolette bringing supplies out for them. They could easily carry enough on their wagon. He was pleased that he'd thought of this because Rose Alice might ask him and he could tell her and she would think he had thought of everything. The fire crackled and he felt the heat soak into his limbs. Outside, a lone wolf howled a long, rising cry. Clay pushed the thought of the Andersons from his mind and moved closer to the fire.

'What about the hundred dollars,' Rose Alice said, 'left from the sale of daddy's farm?'

'Pierre can get it,' Clay said quickly, 'when he and Nicolette come out to join us. We'll lend him a horse and he can ride right back to the bank to fetch it for us. Won't take him no more than a day. He'll do that for us.'

Rose Alice slipped her thumb into her mouth, drew the embroidered flowers close and watched the flames. The heat was suddenly too much for Clay. He stood up and opened the window shutter. Wolves were in the yard. There must have been fifteen of them, maybe more, prowling low and fast, criss-crossing from the cabin to the barn and back trying to pick up a scent. They scratched at the sides of the barn, wheeled and circled and came for the cabin. They scratched and gnawed at the bottom of the door. Inside, Clay and Rose Alice heard the sound of their rasping breath and their claws scraping the wood.

'Pack up what you need,' Clay said.

Clay picked a burning branch out of the fire and opened the door. The wolves scattered and ran back behind trees as he strode across the yard to the barn.

5

Tom Farrow set a bottle and two glasses down on the table nearest the stove and took a seat beside Eli Pitch.

'This ain't the bourbon I usually sell,' Farrow explained. 'I keep it by for when I need to seal an agreement.'

Pitch nodded approval. The men clinked glasses and knocked back their drinks in one. They were the only two people in the saloon. Pitch sat with his back to the stove, blocking the heat.

'How long have you been working for Cumberland, anyway?' Farrow said.

'Don't work for 'em,' Pitch said. 'I'm an independent negotiator. The surveyors write their sssessment reports then the company tells me the land they need to purchase. I negotiate a fee with the land owners and Cumberland pays me commission.'

'So that's what brings you to Vengeance.'

Pitch sat back in his chair.

'The other fella you rode in with,' Farrow said, 'he's your partner?'

Pitch laughed.

'Zeke works for me. We was together in the war, but he ain't reliable. I'll let him go if I can find a business partner here. The Cumberland is interested in the land all along this valley. Would transform the place if they found a seam.'

'Never had us figured for a mining town,' Farrow reflected.

'You've already got a stake here. It would make you a rich man,' Pitch said.

Farrow filled the glasses again.

'Visited the Anderson place and made him an offer yesterday morning,' Pitch said.

'John Anderson?' Farrow said. 'He'll never sell. He built that place.'

Pitch leaned back in his chair.

'Everyone sells,' he said, 'if the offer is right.'

Pitch reached into his waistcoat pocket, brought out a stogie and lit it. He exhaled a stream of blue smoke.

'Anyhow,' he added. 'You can't let a few dirt farmers stand in the way of prosperity. Sometimes I acquire the land myself and sell it to Cumberland that way. 'Course the price is higher because of the investment risk.'

'Cumberland don't mind that?'

'We negotiate,' Pitch said.

A woman's footsteps sounded on the wooden stairs. It was Nicolette. She hesitated when she saw the two men sitting together.

'I've finished upstairs,' she called out to Farrow.

Then she walked quickly out of the saloon without looking at them. Pitch and Farrow watched her. She closed the door behind her.

'Never known a Cajun you could trust,' Pitch said.

'Nicolette's a good worker,' Farrow said.

Pitch sank a second glass of bourbon.

'Town will need protection if the mining company comes,' he said. 'There'll be miners, engineers and company bosses all with money to spend. Might even bring their wives and families if the place is run right.'

Farrow nodded.

'Nobody will make money if it ain't,' Pitch continued. 'I've seen mining towns which are no more than a row of bunkhouses. Nobody's thought of opening a gaming house or a store. If the miners ain't got nothing to spend their money on they send it home. Could be different here.'

Farrow liked this line of argument. He liked order and ambition. He ran his saloon with a sharp eye and had often wished he could run the untidy little farm town in the same way. He had got himself elected as mayor to try to revive the place after the war ended but with genial Jim Parsons as sheriff there was little progress. Only a few farmers made a living from the land; others tried, failed, packed up and joined the wagon trains heading west, believing life would be easy under the Californian sun.

'So what are you saying?'

'You're the mayor. You get me elected sheriff, I'll bring in the mining company and turn Vengeance into a boom town.'

Farrow looked at him. He could almost feel the money in his hands.

'Everyone in town's got a vote,' he said. 'But they'll do what I say.'

He filled their glasses for the third time. Pitch smiled.

'One more thing.'

The men clicked glasses and drank.

'I need to find a couple of guys,' Pitch said. 'Zeke is out lookin' for 'em right now. Names are Butterfield and Choke.'

'Clay and Bill,' Farrow said. 'Their farms are right along from the Anderson place. Clay ain't much of a farmer. He's leaving when the wagon train comes through.'

Pitch's eyes hardened.

'When will that be?'

'Should have left already. Been delayed by this late fall of snow. They aim to start out while the ground's hard.'

'He sold his farm?' Pitch said.

'No one's put an offer in, last I heard,' Farrow said. 'My guess is John Anderson and Bill Choke intend to help themselves to his land as soon as he hits the trail. What's your interest in them anyway?'

'They burned down my house in the war. My family with it.'

'Your family?' Farrow said. 'The 23rd did that?'

Pitch stared at the floor.

'I never heard a story like that.'

'I mean to repay them,' Pitch said. His voice was matter-of-fact. 'Any man would.'

'But something that happened in the war . . . ' Farrow began.

'Who were you with in the war?'

'With Buell until Perryville where I took a bullet. After that, I was excused soldierin'.'

Pitch looked at him coldly.

'Then you are excused commenting on my situation.'

The saloon door crashed open. Zeke York stumbled in and fell on to a chair. His ashen face was tight with pain. The outside of his thigh had been shot away. His hands ran with blood where he tried to hold the wound closed. Farrow and Pitch dashed over to stop him toppling off the chair. They half dragged, half carried him and lay him on the floor in front of the stove. Farrow ran upstairs to fetch a blanket.

Pitch lifted Zeke's head.

'Who did this?'

'I was out at the Butterfield place.'

Zeke's voice was barely a whisper.

'Butterfield did this?'

Zeke's head lolled back in Pitch's hands as consciousness drained from him. Pitch shook him.

'What were you doing? You told me you didn't know where Butterfield lived.'

Zeke groaned.

Farrow appeared with a wool blanket and stuffed a pillow under his head.

'He'll be all right provided he don't bleed to death.'

'You got a doctor in this town?' Pitch demanded.

'I'll fetch Nicolette,' Farrow said. 'She might be able to bandage him up and stop the bleeding. Ain't no doctor for fifty miles.'

Alone with Zeke again, Pitch grasped his head with both hands and shook him.

'What were you doing out there?' he snarled. 'I told you to find out where he was and leave the rest to me.'

Zeke opened his eyes and groaned. Pitch shook him again.

'You were trying to cut a deal for yourself and got shot. Did you get the deeds?'

He dropped Zeke's head back on to the thin pillow and got to his feet.

Outside, Zeke's horse was tethered at the rail. Pitch went through both saddle-bags, but there was nothing which interested him. As Farrow and Nicolette ran towards him down the street, Pitch stepped back inside. Zeke was lying with his eyes closed. A film of sweat covered his face and his breathing was shallow.

'I should shoot you now,' Pitch hissed. 'Ain't nobody double crosses me.'

The saloon door burst open again.

'Boil some water,' Nicolette said. 'There's dirt in the wound.'

★   ★   ★

When he saw the smoke, 12-year-old John Anderson Junior knew something was wrong. From up here in the woods, he could see black smoke climbing across the pale sky but the trees grew close together and there was no view of the valley. He could cut back down, but that would mean neglecting most of his traps. The ones he had looked at so far had all been empty. His father would laugh at him if he went home after being out all day with nothing to show for it. There was a ridge half a mile higher. He would be able to see from there. Then he could check on the traps on the way down. Strange. His father hadn't said anything about building a fire before he left. That sort of job was usually left to him. He pushed on up the slope.

John Junior didn't usually come this way and the undergrowth was thicker than he expected. Thorns tore at his clothing, the ground was steep and his legs ached. When he got to the ridge, the view wasn't as good as he'd remembered either. He could see the valley floor two miles away, the wide sky and the horizon but the land in the lee of the hillside where their house stood was still hidden from his view. Strands of black smoke blew across the sky, but it was not a thick column like before. This lessened John Junior's anxiety. If there had been trouble, it had passed.

The light was fading when he had visited all his traps and started home.

The detour had made him late and he knew his mother worried if he was in the woods after dark. That would mean a telling off. To make matters worse, the traps had all been empty, so his father was sure to laugh at him and he hated that. He dawdled, stopped to pick up sticks and sling them into the under-growth where they landed with a satisfying crash.

So what if he was late? So what if the traps had been empty? So what if his mother was worried? He didn't have go home at all if he didn't want to. What was the point, if all they were going to do was laugh at him and be angry with him? He could stay here in the woods all night if he wanted to. He knew how to build a fire, there was bound to be something in one of the traps in the morning. He could live out here for days. That's what he would do. He'd stay out here for days until they forgot about laughing at him and being angry with him and were just pleased to see him. He'd walk in the door, the room would be filled with the smell of his mother's baking, there would be food waiting for him on the table and his pa would be sitting in his chair by the fire with his box of lures open on his knee. No one would scold or laugh at him at all.

Food. He was always hungry but remembering the smell of his mother's baking made him ravenous. He felt in his pocket just to check, but he knew he'd eaten his last piece of hard tack hours ago. And there was a smell in the air, bitter and dark. It was getting stronger as he made his way down the slope. He couldn't tell what it was; he hadn't noticed it higher up but it was everywhere now and caught in his throat like dirt. Smoke. It was the smell of something burning. An old fire which had not quite died.

Light was fading now. John Junior hurried down the lower slopes. He remembered that there were wolves in the valley and suddenly, more than anything else, he wanted to be home.

He stumbled over roots and branches whipped his face but it didn't matter. All those thoughts about staying out in the woods had flown from his head. He didn't care about being told off any more. He just wanted to be back inside in the warm with his ma and his pa there. He didn't even care if he had missed his supper, although hunger turned in his belly like a claw.

John Junior broke through the last line of trees on to the sloping pasture which led down to the farm and started to run. Grey light surrounded him. It was a relief to be out of the shadows of the woods, but there was this terrible stench in the air. And then he stopped still. The house was gone. And the barn. There were just black, charred ruins where buildings had stood that morning. And he knew that the smell which had been so familiar and yet so strong it had been impossible to recognize, was the smell of his home burning.

Thoughts collided in his head so they weren't so much thoughts as things he was looking at and couldn't recognize, even though he knew what they were. There was space where his house had been. Where the barn had stood, there was emptiness. His legs were suddenly weak and he sat down in the snow. Smoke rose from the ruins.

Where was his ma? Where was his pa? What had happened? How could this have happened? And then he saw them. Lying in the snow only fifteen yards away. Someone had piled blackened timbers on them. But he could see them clearly underneath. What on earth were they doing? He lifted some of the wood away. It was strange because they were lying face down and neither of them was wearing a coat. He would have been scolded if he had lain down in the snow even if he had been wearing a coat. Their skin was whiter than he had ever seen which made them look unlike themselves and there was snow in their hair. And then the understanding came into his head that they were dead.

John Junior saw the blood which stained the back of his father's shirt and the back of his mother's dress. He spoke to them then very softly but urgently, as if they were sleeping and he wanted to wake them. He said their names just loud enough for them to hear. Even though he knew they would not answer, he waited for them to reply. Of course they did not. And that was also strange to him.

And then there was nothing. John Junior did not cry or cry out. He stood there staring. Wanting to touch his mother and father and not wanting to. The light was fading round him. Darkness was moving out of the woods across the open valley. Everything was silent. There was no wind, no cries from the screech owls. Just the smoke rising up from the chaos of burned timber. He looked around him. The corral fences were broken down and the horses were gone.

Then a small movement caught his eye. A lone rider was climbing the hill to the west, the route they took to Bill Choke's place. But it wasn't Bill. Even though the rider was far away, he knew that. But he couldn't tell who it was. The rider was almost at the top. There was no point in calling out; the rider wouldn't be able to hear from this distance. Then another thought came into his head. He shouldn't call out. This was the man. The rider was the man who had done this. He had burned the house and the barn and shot his ma and pa and covered them with wood. Now he was riding away. Without understanding quite why, John Junior started to follow him.

Forgetting how hungry he was or how cold or that night was closing in, John Junior kept his eyes on the rider and stumbled after him through the snow. The rider did not pause or look back. John Junior had not thought what he would do if the man noticed him. He had no choice. He had to follow him to find out who he was. He had to get closer or he would lose sight of him as darkness fell.

There were only three places the rider could be going: Bill Choke's place, the Butterfields' or on into town. Bill Choke's was the most likely. It would soon be too dark to ride much further. John Junior lost sight of the rider as he crossed the brow of the hill. He tried to make himself run, but the muscles in his legs burned and he was weak from lack of food. He felt in his pocket again just to be certain there was no hard tack left. And he was thirsty. His throat was parched. He reached down and scooped up a handful of snow, without slackening his pace.

At the top of the hill he stopped to catch his breath and to snatch up another handful of snow. He stuffed some in his mouth and rubbed a handful over his face and round the back of his neck. The rider's outline was faint now, barely a shadow in the failing light. But he had stopped, hadn't he? John Junior strained his eyes. The rider was waiting for something. Was he looking back? Maybe he had realized he was being followed.

Then there was a spark and a tiny red glow, which came and went in the darkness. The rider had lit a cigarette. John Junior hurried on down the snowy hillside. He wouldn't lose him now. Lights from Bill Choke's house shone out over the snow. He had lit torches to keep the wolves away from the door. The flames reared and danced in the darkness. The rider carried on past the entrance. On towards Butterfield's and the town. Then there was a neat arc of sparks as he flicked the end of his cigarette away into the snow. John Junior had nothing to guide him now.

Further down the valley, there were wolves behind the treeline. They were calling out to each other, long, lonesome howls. John Junior had listened to the wolves most winter nights of his life, call and answer across the empty snow. He could hear them now moving amongst the trees, pausing to howl into the night. They were shadowing the rider. And the rider had heard them too. His horse's hoof beats had picked up speed.

6

John Anderson Junior hung back as the rider turned into the Butterfield place. Clay Butterfield? Was that who the rider was? His pa had known Clay for years. They had served together during the war.

Thoughts exploded in John Junior's head. He remembered how Bill Choke and his pa always laughed about Clay. They said he was such a lousy shot that they had to make him a bugler in the army. When his hogs died last winter, they said they'd been sick when he bought them, anyone could have told him. When his calf was killed by the wolves, they said he'd made history: that had never happened in the valley before. They said his wife had been driven plumb crazy by what had happened in the war. They said, if Clay didn't look after her better, she'd die.

And what kind of man couldn't look after his own wife? They'd laughed about that too.

Then John Junior understood. Clay was jealous because his pa was better than him. He looked after his family. He was a good farmer. Their horses would fetch a high price come the spring, he had heard his pa say so.

Get the sheriff. That's what he had to do. He turned and started to run back up the track to the Vengeance road. He forgot how tired he was and that he had just walked four miles and had not eaten for hours. As he reached the road he heard gunshots from the Butterfield place. Who was Clay Butterfield shooting now?

Clouds moved and uncovered the moon. A ribbon of muddy track stretched ahead through the silver landscape. He slowed to a walk. Pain burned in his side. Somewhere, back towards the Butterfield place, a wolf howled and another answered.

Then terror. Hoofbeats behind him.

A rider was coming. Clay Butterfield had seen him and was coming after him. Maybe he had known all along that John Junior was following him. He was on a killing spree. He had killed his ma and pa; he had probably killed Bill Choke and those shots meant he had probably killed his crazy wife. John Junior looked around for somewhere to hide. There was nowhere, no trees on this stretch of road, only snow and shadows. Maybe if he lay down, Clay wouldn't see him. John Junior ran off the road and threw himself down in a patch of mud. In a second, his clothes were soaked through and ice entered his veins.

With his face flat on the frozen ground, he watched the rider approach. He was slumped low in the saddle and clutched the pommel awkwardly. John Junior needn't have worried. The man rode straight past without looking in his direction at all. He lay where he was until he could no longer hear hoof beats. His whole body was frozen numb. When he pushed himself to his feet, his limbs felt so stiff and brittle he thought his feet might snap off at the ankles. Slowly, he put one foot in front of the other, willing himself to keep going. He remembered Sheriff Parsons' cheerful face. He had been in the same unit as his pa too. He would help him. He would know what to do.

* * *

Since the war, Rose Alice was terrified of most things. Every night in her dreams, she defended herself against fire and attack. When she was awake the thing she feared most was wolves. As the wagon lurched over the frozen ground in the moonlight, she knew wolves were following. She sat out front so that she could keep watch, even though the air was freezing. Clay said they wouldn't attack but she didn't believe him. He often told lies to stop her worrying. She pulled the blanket tighter round her.

'Wolves will follow the scent of the goat, won't they, Clay?'

'They might,' Clay said. 'But we ain't leaving him.'

The goat was tethered to their bedpost in the back of the wagon beside the crate of chickens.

'Why don't you go back there and get some sleep?' Clay said. 'Then I could take a turn.'

'Ain't you worried about no one coming after us?'

'They ain't gonna come after us while it's dark,' Clay said.

The wagon jolted. Rose Alice clung to the side of her seat.

'If I go to sleep, I'll have that dream again.'

'Dreams can't hurt you,' Clay said.

A wolf howled somewhere back in the direction of the farm and another answered. Rose Alice moved closer to Clay.

'Always the same dream,' Rose Alice said. 'The night them Johnny Rebs came.'

'Think about California,' Clay said. 'Maybe you'll dream about sunshine.'

'Did you put in my hatchet?'

Clay laughed.

'You're the only person I know that can't sleep unless they're holding on to a hatchet. I reckon we should get a doll and you could hold on to that like you did when you were a girl. When we get to California, I could carve one for you out of wood. I bet they have cotton-wood out there, real soft and easy to carve.'

Rose Alice slipped her arm out from under the blanket, put her thumb in her mouth and imagined the doll Clay would make for her when they got to California. The wagon pitched left and right over the unforgiving ground. A wolf howled, closer this time.

'Maybe I could carve dolls and we could sell 'em,' Clay said.

Rose Alice tucked her arm inside the blanket again. She shook her head violently.

'You don't know what dolls are like,'

she said. 'You wouldn't know how to do that.'

'Why not?' Clay said. 'I carved that candlestick didn't I?'

'Dolls have their own ways,' Rose Alice explained. 'Just like people. Everyone of 'em's different.'

The wagon jolted again and nearly pitched them off the seat. The tortured cry of a screech owl split the night. Clay flicked the reins.

'I could make the clothes,' Rose Alice said. 'I watched my ma do that.'

'That's right,' Clay said. 'You could do that.'

'Jonny Rebs burned my dolls alive,' Rose Alice said sadly. 'Everyone of 'em. There wasn't nothing I could do 'cept listen to 'em screamin'. You want to know what happened after that?'

'Think about the sunshine,' Clay said. 'Think of all that sunshine we're gonna get in California. Sunshine every day. We can just sit there an' it'll be warm an' nice an' we won't even have to wear coats nor wrap ourselves in blankets neither.'

'You want to know? There was two of 'em.'

'We could just sit in the sunshine an' nothing would matter. We wouldn't have no worries, no one would bother us and we would just sit side by side, warm as two loaves just took out of the oven.'

Rose Alice slipped her thumb back into her mouth as the picture of sunshine which Clay had conjured, filled her head. Ahead of them, the moon lit the snowy range.

★ ★ ★

The man had lost a lot of blood and kept fainting, but he would recover. Kneeling beside him, Nicolette bathed the wound, pinched out any buckshot she could see and cut up a cotton sheet for a bandage. As she worked, Pitch and Tom Farrow carried on with their conversation as if she wasn't there.

'Can't wait for no election,' Pitch

said. 'I'll ride out to the Butterfield place in the morning.'

He looked down at Zeke and nudged him with the toe of his boot.

'You're a damn fool for getting yourself shot.'

Zeke groaned.

'Don't have to be elected,' Farrow said. 'As mayor, I can appoint you honorary sheriff right now. Then you can act with the full force of the law.'

Pitch laughed.

'I like that.'

'We can hold the election later.'

Nicolette tied the last strip of bandage.

'He needs a bed to rest on,' she said. 'We should carry him upstairs.'

Pitch dug him in the ribs with the toe of his boot.

'Can't he walk?'

Zeke groaned again.

Tom Farrow reached down and pulled Zeke's arm over his shoulder and hauled him to his feet. Nicolette took the other arm and together they got him upstairs. Pitch sipped his bourbon.

As soon as she left the saloon, Nicolette headed for the stable and saddled her horse. She filled a canteen, wrapped a hunk of bread in a piece of cloth and stuffed it into a saddlebag. She took the Winchester and put on Pierre's saddle jacket, scarf and hat and rode out. Leaving now, she would be at Clay and Rose Alice's farm by two in the morning, sooner if the moon was full.

Hours later when the moon emerged from behind a cloud, she passed a body face down on the ground a few yards from the side of the road. The sight shocked her, but with the warning she had to give Clay and Rose Alice uppermost in her mind, she rode past without stopping. What could she do for a corpse? Maybe he had been in a gunfight with the man whose leg she had bandaged back at the saloon. But the image of the body stayed in her head.

A mile further on, Nicolette heard

the long high howl of a wolf. There was a full moon now and the night air was freezing. She pulled the collar of her jacket tighter. She had to turn back. She had to check to see if he was dead or alive, whoever he was. She pulled on the reins.

Nicolette knew she had remembered the place correctly. But the corpse was gone. She looked up and down the road, rode off the track and scanned the dark horizon. Nothing. A wolf howled again and the answering call was close by. Nicolette had rarely known fear and wasn't afraid now, but she felt weak without Pierre beside her and the place unsettled her. Had she imagined the body beside the road? And why had she allowed herself to ride past? She reached behind her to let her hand rest on the stock of the Winchester for a moment. She clicked her tongue and rode on.

Nicolette knew the Butterfield place was empty as soon as she rode into the yard. She hallooed without expecting a reply. When she pushed open the cabin door, everything was gone, even the furniture. Cold ashes lay in the grate. Then dread seized her. She ran out to the barn and flung open the door. The wagon was gone, the horses were gone, even the barrel of feed. Rats scuffled in the straw. When she entered the cabin again, she was shaking. Her friends had deserted her.

There was kindling and logs beside the grate. Don't think about it. Make a fire. She made herself concentrate on the simple task which she had carried out a thousand times. She brought more logs in from the pile outside the cabin door. She could hear wolves moving behind the trees; her horse shifted uneasily. She unhitched her and led her into the cabin and pulled the door closed.

With her horse tethered inside, the fire lit and her Winchester within easy reach, Nicolette felt safe. She sat down by the fire, tore off a hunk of sourdough bread and took a swig of water from her canteen. Then she allowed herself to think. They'd left her behind. It didn't make sense but there it was. Pierre and Clay had spent all winter planning the journey. They deliberated over the best time to travel, whether to join a train coming up from the south or push out alone. They talked about what they would need, how Pierre and Nicolette would pick up work through the winter and add their money to the hundred dollars Clay and Rose Alice had saved. Why hadn't they waited for her?

There was a scratching at the door. Nicolette reached for the Winchester. Her horse shifted uneasily. She got up, kicked the door and heard the wolves scatter. She opened one of the shutters. A wolf pack patrolled the yard. Why hadn't Rose Alice and Clay waited for her? The question cartwheeled in her brain. What should she do? What would Pierre have done? The fire crackled and black shadows reared across the ceiling.

Nicolette rested the Winchester across her knees, unbuttoned her jacket and leaned back against the wall. Minutes later, she was asleep and dreaming she was standing alone in the middle of the prairie with a storm wind rushing round her and clouds dashing overhead.

★　★　★

John Anderson Junior thought he was going to die from the cold. He had had to throw himself down on the freezing, soaking ground again when the second rider came past. This time the rider was heading out of town. But he couldn't take any chances: Clay Butterfield knew he had discovered his series of murders; he was looking for him. He'd ridden all the way to Vengeance, discovered that John Junior wasn't there and was retracing his steps. Clay must want to kill him really bad.

Walking forward into the night, John Junior found a stick by the roadside which he could use to help himself along, like an old man with a cane. He was so cold and tired he didn't care about anything now. He just kept going and going. Going and going. When the wolves howled, he howled back. When one got within sight of the road, he threw stones at it, more for sport than to drive it away. Sometimes he sang out loud. Mad, made up songs with nonsense words and melodies no musician would recognize.

Everything hurt, his whole body, except the parts that were numb with cold. Pain burned in his side. Fire tortured the muscles in his legs. He had lost all feeling in his feet hours before and his hands were frozen. Worst of all was the slab of cold which lay across his chest where he had thrown himself down when the riders came. His ribcage had been broken open and filled with ice.

He had no idea where he was. He was just somewhere on the road to Vengeance. How far he had come or had left to go, he did not know. He wondered if it was possible to sleep and walk at the same time and tried walking with his eyes closed to see if he could get some sleep that way, but he veered off the track and fell over. He knew he'd cut himself but he couldn't feel anything because his knees were numb. And he didn't want to get up. The frozen ground was as welcoming as his warm straw mattress back home. As he lay there in the moonlight listening to the wolves howl, the thought floated into his head that if he was asleep and the wolves came, they could eat him and he wouldn't even know it.

7

'You're forgetting something,' Farrow called.

The grey clouds of the previous days had gone. A bright afternoon sun shone in the pale sky and promised warmth. Thawing snow dripped from the roof of the saloon.

Eli Pitch and Zeke were mounted and ready to ride out. Pitch's hat was pulled down low against the sunlight. Zeke's face was tight with pain.

Farrow ran down the steps from the saloon with a sheriffs tin star in his hand.

Pitch leaned down to allow him to pin the badge on his lapel.

'You sure he's fit enough to ride?' Farrow nodded towards Zeke.

'He's got to cover my back,' Pitch said.

'Clay won't give you no trouble,'

Farrow said. 'Couldn't hit a barn door if he was aiming right at it.'

'Anyhow, I want him with me or he might be tempted to go off and make deals on his own.'

Pitch wheeled his horse round and clicked his tongue for the horse to ride on. Zeke followed a few steps behind.

Zeke's concentration was taken up with his wound and he appeared not to hear them. A mile out of town, the pain was too much.

'Hold up,' he called.

The men reined in their horses. Zeke shifted in the saddle to relieve the pressure on his leg. Pitch admired his tin star.

'Hurts like hell,' Zeke said.

Pitch held up his hand to show the two missing fingers.

'That's what hurts-like-hell looks like.'

Zeke grimaced. His face was as pale as the scar which slashed his cheek.

'Shouldn't have been out there in the first place,' Pitch continued. 'Should have waited for me.'

'Should you have been where you was when you lost them fingers?'

Pitch glared at him. 'That was war.'

'War was an excuse for the things you done,' Zeke said.

Pitch turned away and spurred his horse on. Patches of snow were strewn across the valley sides like pieces of cloud which had fallen from the sky. The muddy track towards the three farms ran east into the sun and the men shielded their eyes. Away to the south, they had a view over miles of prairie and they could just make out a line of covered wagons advancing across the horizon. Pitch pointed to them. Zeke drew his horse level with Pitch's.

'Don't you ever say nothin' about the war to me,' Pitch said. 'You know what I lost.'

'I know,' Zeke said.

'Anyhow, you were with me. You did the same things I did.'

Zeke grimaced as the pain burned in his leg. The men rode on in silence.

From a distance they thought it was a heap of old sacks at the foot of the hackberry. As they got closer, they realized it was a body. Frost glistened on the clothes. Zeke slid down from his saddle; Pitch drew his gun and dismounted. They approached warily. A black vulture circled above them.

Pitch kicked the heap of clothes with the toe of his boot. There was no response. Zeke uncovered the face. It was a boy, not much more than twelve years old. The vulture landed a few yards away and watched them.

'He's breathin',' Zeke said. 'He'll be froze to the bone if he's been out here all night.'

Zeke hauled the boy to his feet. Pitch holstered his gun and leaned forward to grab the boy's arm.

'His clothes is soaking wet,' Zeke said.

John Junior opened his eyes. The first thing he saw was the tin star pinned to Pitch's coat.

'Sheriff Parsons?'

His voice was faint.

The men held him between them and made him walk a few steps to try to restore some circulation.

'You running away from somethin', boy?' Pitch said.

'Sheriff Parsons?' John Junior said.

'He ain't seeing right,' Zeke said.

'Clay Butterfield shot my ma and pa and burned our house.'

The boy's voice was thin and rasped in this throat. The men strained to listen.

'I followed him.'

They sat John Junior down and leaned him against the hackberry trunk. Zeke fetched his canteen and put it to his lips.

'What's your name, kid?' Pitch said.

'I was in the woods tendin' my traps. I followed him back to his farm. He shot his wife.'

The boy's head lolled back against the tree. His eyes closed.

'He don't know what he's sayin',' Zeke said. 'Being out in the cold all night has given him brain fever.'

Pitch dug him in the ribs with the toe of his boot. The boy's eyes opened again.

'What's your name?'

The vulture hopped closer.

'We should try to get him warm,' Zeke said.

'Sheriff Parsons,' John Junior said. 'Is that you?'

Pitch leaned down and put his face close.

'I asked you. What's your name?'

'John Anderson Junior.'

Pitch stood up and looked at Zeke.

'Get back on your horse.'

'You ain't Sheriff Parsons,' John Junior said.

Pitch drew his Colt and shot John Junior in the chest. A patch of blood blossomed through his ragged clothes. The vulture screeched and bounced away a few yards. The sound of the shot echoed across the empty sky.

As the men rode away, the sun warmed the air. Pitch loosened his scarf and undid his jacket. The light twinkled on his silver Colt.

'Would have died anyway,' Pitch said. 'I just hurried it along.'

'My leg hurts like hellfire,' Zeke said.

'Can't afford no more stops if we want to get there before dark.'

The hoofs of their horses splashed on through the mud.

* * *

Dusk gathered as the two riders turned off the track to Clay Butterfield's place. They dismounted in the shadows beneath the tulip poplars and kept their eyes on the cabin. Smoke rose from the chimney but there was no horse tethered to the rail outside. At the far end of the yard, the barn door was half open, but they couldn't see into the dark interior. Wolf tracks were printed in the mud.

Keeping back in the shadows beneath the trees and with a clear sight of the cabin door, the men drew their weapons.

'Clay Butterfield!' Pitch shouted.

There was no answer and stillness descended on the yard.

'Clay Butterfield!' Pitch yelled again.

A woman's voice came from inside the cabin.

'He ain't here.'

'You his wife?'

'No I ain't. Who are you?'

'Eli Pitch, Sheriff of Vengeance.'

There was a pause.

'Guess you know you ain't welcome here, Eli Pitch, or you would have come right up and knocked on the door.'

A window shutter swung open and the barrel of a Winchester pointed towards the men. Pitch and Zeke scrambled to take cover behind the trees.

'Ain't you I've come to see, lady. My business is with Butterfield.'

'I've told you he ain't here.'

'I know that voice,' Zeke whispered. 'The Cajun. From the saloon.'

'Mind telling me where he is?' Pitch called.

A shot from the Winchester nicked the branch an inch above Pitch's head and showered him with splinters.

The two men threw themselves to the ground and crawled back behind the stand of trees. Zeke cursed and clutched his wounded leg.

'Tell us where he is and we'll leave right now,' Pitch called again.

Another rifle shot ricocheted off the trees.

'She ain't going to tell us,' Zeke said. 'Let's go.'

The men led their horses over a rise, out of sight of the house. The pale colours of the day had darkened across the landscape and the air was chill. Pillows of snow lay under the trees.

'Must have taken his wagon and gone off to join the train,' Zeke said. 'Where else would he have gone?'

'Why is she still here?' Pitch said. 'She's supposed to have gone with him.'

'Maybe she's wants to stay here now, take on the farm.'

Pitch laced the reins of his horse

107

around a tree branch.

'She's got a wagon in town, she's planning on joining the train too.'

He drew his Colt and checked the chamber.

'If she don't show up at the train, then Butterfield is gonna come lookin' for her.'

Zeke leaned on his saddle to take the weight off his leg.

'I got to get inside where I can lay down in the warm. I shouldn't never have come out here.'

Shadows filled the spaces between the trees; stars began to show through the evening sky. Pitch climbed the ridge to get a view of the cabin. Smoke climbed from the chimney and firelight showed through the cracks in the shutters. Pitch strained his eyes. The barn door was half open as before.

'She's smarter than we are,' Zeke said. 'She's on the inside and we're on the outside. We're the ones gonna freeze to death.'

Pitch crossed the rise and stood

beneath the poplars.

'Lady,' he called. 'I'm offerin' you a trade. We got food and coffee out here. You can have a share if you'll let us warm ourselves by your fire.'

The shutter swung open again and the barrel of the Winchester jabbed towards the trees. A shot ripped through the branches. Then the rifle barrel withdrew and the shutter slammed.

Pitch crossed the rise to where Zeke was still supporting himself by holding on to his saddle.

'If we bed down in the barn, she can get a direct shot at us,' Pitch said. 'Best make a fire here.'

The men found enough dry kindling beneath the trees. They sat close to the fire and waited for the coffee to boil. Zeke stretched out his injured leg. The wound had opened and blood stained the leg of his pants.

'We'll keep the horses saddled,' Pitch said. 'Reckon she'll make a run for it in the night.'

'Ground's wet,' Zeke said. He leaned

back against the trunk of a poplar. 'I hate sleepin' on wet ground.'

A wolf howled somewhere far off. The horses shifted uneasily.

'Can't decide whether to shoot her or keep her alive,' Pitch said. 'If we shoot her, Butterfield will come lookin' for her and we can shoot him too. If we keep her alive, he'll still come lookin' and we can trade her for the deeds to this place. Then we can shoot 'em both. Not much difference in it.'

'I hate sleepin' out at this time of year,' Zeke said. 'You sit by the fire, your front burns while there's frost layin' down your back. Got to keep turning like a pig on a spit.'

He eased himself round until he had his back to the fire.

'If you're doin' that, you can keep watch while I get some shuteye,' Pitch said. He leaned back against a tree stump and pulled his hat down over his face.

'Know what?' Pitch said, from underneath his hat. 'I told that fool mayor I was an independent agent for the mining company. He believed me.'

'Yeah?'

Light from the fire danced among the lower branches of the trees. To the other side of them, where the open fields were, darkness walled them in. The stars had disappeared and there was no moon. They could hear the light steps and the harsh breath of wolves as they ran back and forth on the open ground. The horses moved uneasily.

'You didn't have to shoot that kid,' Zeke said.

Pitch pushed his hat off his face.

'He was Anderson's kid. He would have had a claim on the farm. Besides that, you know the other reason we come here. I'm gonna take everything these guys got because of what they did.'

'What you say they did,' Zeke said. 'You ain't never had proof.'

Pain flayed his leg and made him catch his breath.

'You saw my farm. Fields black as

hell. House burned down. And the barn.'

'I saw that,' Zeke said. 'But I never saw no bodies. And nor did you. Way I figure it is your old lady took off when she heard the Yankees was comin'. If she ain't come back, it means she don't want to.'

'I should shoot you right now for saying that.'

A sound amongst the trees made them both look up. A footstep? The horses stamped their feet. The men slipped their Colts out of their holsters and peered into the shadows. The more they stared, the more they doubted they had heard anything. There were sounds but they were the rustling of animals, the tread of the horses, the crack and spit of the fire. Pitch stood up and walked a few yards out into the darkness to where he could see the firelight behind the shutters on the cabin windows. The sight reassured him as, if the fire was still lit, Nicolette must still be there.

Then both men heard the oiled,

metallic snick of a Winchester being cocked. They jumped to their feet, stared wildly out of the ring of firelight into the darkness. They each turned their backs on the flames and faced opposite directions, Colts ready. There was another footstep, away to the left but close. They waved their Colts, scanning the darkness. The horses whinnied, sensing their unease.

Another sound. Someone clicked their tongue as if they were telling a horse to move on. More movement amongst their horses. Then a rifle shot exploded the coffee pot, which had been balancing on the fire between them. A cloud of steam burst as the coffee splashed the flames. Both men yelled. They fired blind into the darkness, shot after shot until the chambers of their Colts were empty. When quiet returned, they heard the hoof beats of their terrified horses galloping away into the night.

8

Bill Choke woke at first light with Clay's story about the Confederate renegade on his mind. It was just like Butterfield to panic over a story like that and come running to him or John; he had been trailing after them since he was a kid. Nevertheless, Bill figured he ought to let John know.

John Anderson loved to shoot and if there was one thing which made him down tools and come riding over the crest of the hill, it was the sound of Bill Choke's shotgun when he was out hunting quail. Unusually, Anderson had not shown up the previous day even though Choke had been out with his gun for hours.

What could some embittered Confederate want with them now? Choke racked his brains. He had done things in the war which he was not proud of.

Both sides had. And when those memories came to him, he pushed them aside. The war was over; he was home. He had fought hard, not for any ideology, just to defend what was his. This part of Kentucky was Union territory so he fought for the Union.

Bill Choke knew he was one of the lucky ones: he had returned home to find his farm untouched and his wife waiting. He was a practical man and knew the future held promise. As he settled back into civilian life, he sometimes joked that all he had to show for his years in the army was a pair of Colts and a French clock but he knew he had more than that. He had his old life back.

That morning everything changed.

From the brow of the hill, Bill Choke saw the blackened ruins of the Anderson house and the group of vultures pecking at something halfway up the slope to the woods. When he got down to the house he waved his arms and shouted to scare off the birds but they only hopped a few yards away and eyed him with confident malevolence. He knew the mutilated corpses were John and Amy by the ribbons of their clothes. They were half covered by charred timbers from the house as if someone had built a funeral pyre but only the wood had burned and not the bodies. Choke turned away and gagged on the bile which rose in his throat. This was no accident. He just hoped they had died quickly. Telling himself he was searching for clues, Choke rode round the remains of the house but found nothing. There were hoof prints in the mud. What could they tell him?

Heading back up the hill towards his own farm, Choke's hands could barely grip the reins and there was water in his belly. He knew that as soon as he was a few yards away, the vultures would return to feed. He did not look back.

Should he ride into town to inform Sheriff Parsons or should he stay at home to defend his own place? He could hardly leave Ellen alone. A picture appeared in his head of Amy Anderson's body with pieces of its flesh torn away from the bones. Choke grabbed the pommel of his saddle to steady himself. He could take his wife into town with him, but that would mean leaving the farm deserted. If there was no one there, it would be an invitation. He would leave her his shotgun and all his shells.

An overwhelming feeling of relief swept through him when Bill Choke saw his own house again. There was smoke rising from the chimney and he could make out Ellen sweeping the porch. Otto tore down the track to greet him and ran in furious, joyous circles round him and his horse. Bill Choke's father had cleared the land and built the house. Bill had added fences and a corral. This spring he would buy a foal, rear her and breed from her. As soon as Butterfield left for California he planned to take over his land, plough it and sow spring corn. Then he remembered the blackened ruins of

Anderson's place. That would be vacant now too. And the thought came to him that, if he made the right moves, he could end up farming the whole valley. He could join his farm with Anderson's, have a lawyer draw up the deeds and take Anderson's boy to live with them as payment. It would be perfect.

Ellen Choke took the broom back inside and closed the door as he approached. He tethered his horse on the porch rail and followed her. Otto jumped up at him, panting and thrashing the air with his tail. Choke told Ellen briefly what he had seen and that he intended to ride into town to inform Sheriff Parsons.

'Amy too?'

The sight of bones stripped of flesh came back into Choke's head.

'I didn't see a sign of John Junior.'

Ellen Choke sank down into a chair.

'I'll be back early tomorrow,' Choke said. 'You'll have the shotgun and Otto.'

He left his wife staring out of the window over the empty fields while he went into the kitchen in search of a bone for Otto.

'I suppose you'll be wantin' to take on John's place now,' Ellen said.

'I ain't considered it,' Choke said.

Ellen watched her husband stoop down and talk softly to the dog.

★　★　★

By sunset, Nicolette had finished loading the wagon. She collected the wages Tom Farrow owed her and paid her bills at the store and livery stable. The wagon train would be there in the morning. They would want to stay in town for a few days but she couldn't wait; she had to get out of town before Eli Pitch found his way back. 'Ain't advisable,' Sam Logan said, when she told him she intended to start out right away. Logan ran the livery stable and had seen many wagon trains go through.

'You're overloaded as it is. The way you'll be goin', the ground is real rough. If you lose a wheel, who's gonna help you?'

'Got to get a head start,' Nicolette said. 'The train will only be a couple of days behind me.'

Sam led the horses out of the stable and helped Nicolette with the harnesses.

'Got a shotgun for the wolves?' he said.

Nicolette pulled her jacket tight round her. A blood-red sunset rested on the horizon.

'Aim for that,' Sam said. 'Keep going straight.'

Nicolette jerked the reins and the wagon moved off. She had been expecting Pitch to show up at any moment ever since she had been back in town. If she could just get a mile or two out on to the prairie, darkness would hide her for the night. She kept the Winchester on the seat beside her.

The wagon creaked and lurched. The last time Nicolette had sat on this seat, Pierre had been beside her. Remembering his sweet face, she felt a knife turn within her and for a while she could hardly sit up straight. But Pierre would have wanted her to do this. He would have wanted her to go on. A new life in California was the dream they shared. She knew there should be comfort in that thought but she could not find it.

Nicolette could see her way clearly by moonlight. The prairie grass looked like the waves of a frozen sea. She got used to the creak and lurch of the wagon. When she first set out, Sam's warning about the uneven ground rang in her ears and she feared the next jolt would loosen a wheel. But gradually she forgot it. The wagon was strong and the horses were unperturbed by the rough ground. She heard the howl of wolves and the cry of screech owls but neither concerned her. Every turn of the wheels took her closer to California.

Then Nicolette heard the sound she most dreaded: hoof beats approaching from the direction of the town. Her heart exploded. She felt for the Winchester and craned round the side of the wagon but couldn't make out anyone. The drumming hoofs were getting louder. She moved across the seat and peered round the other side of the wagon. There were two of them.

Nicolette grabbed the Winchester, clambered over the back of the seat and crouched behind the tailboard. The riders were heading straight for her. She squinted along the barrel of the rifle and waited for them to come within range. Then something made her hesitate. What if it wasn't Pitch? One of them was in her sights now. How could she be sure? It could be Sam or even Tom Farrow. It could even be someone from the wagon train riding out to find her. She lowered the rifle. As she did so, she saw the riders part.

At first Nicolette thought they were riding round something. Then she realized they were going to approach the wagon from different sides. She fired, but the shot went wide. One of the riders was holding his Colt. A stream of lead hammered into the tailboard of the wagon. She fired back but didn't have time to aim.

Then someone was up front and climbing on to the driver's seat. She turned and fired the Winchester wildly. The wagon was piled with furniture and she didn't have a clear view. Her shots tore the canvas. She felt the wagon slowing and heard a man's voice calling a 'Woah', to the horses. Then someone grabbed her from behind, tore the Winchester out of her hands and twisted her arms behind her until her sinews cracked.

'Find me something to tie her with,' Pitch yelled.

Nicolette craned round to spit in his face. He wrenched her arms up behind her until she thought they would snap like kindling. Then he heaved her out over the tailboard. Stars burst in her head as she hit the ground.

The two men tied Nicolette's arms behind her. Bruised and disorientated from her fall, she was barely able to struggle. She sat on the ground and her head span.

'We gonna make her walk?' Zeke said.

'We'll take the horses. She can ride one. We'll freeze to death if we go back at walking pace.'

Zeke began to unhitch the pair.

Pitch jabbed her with the toe of his boot.

'Took us three hours to find our horses,' he said. 'You're lucky we don't shoot you right now and leave you here for the wolves.'

Nicolette ignored him and turned away. She looked west in the direction she had been travelling. The empty grassland rolled ahead. Her dreams lay out there somewhere.

'You listening?'

Pitch kicked her.

'Last person that pointed a Winchester at me is lyin' six feet below right now. Think yourself lucky.'

Zeke brought over the horses.

'We gonna leave the wagon here?'

He put his arms round Nicolette to lift her on to the horse. She wrenched herself away from him and kicked out. When he tried again she jabbed her head sideways and broke his nose. Zeke howled with pain and clutched his face. Blood spilled through his fingers.

Pitch drew his gun and pressed the barrel into the side of Nicolette's neck. He clicked back the hammer and the chamber turned.

'I'm gonna put you on that horse,' he said. 'You struggle and I'll turn you into crow bait.'

He heaved her up on to the horse like a sack.

'You wait till I got you in a jail cell,' Zeke spat. 'I got a way of dealin' with you.'

Pitch took the reins to Nicolette's horse and the three of them turned towards town.

★　★　★

The saloon was packed out. Every seat was taken. Townsfolk lined the walls and crowded around the door. Tom Farrow had taken on Sam Logan as barkeep for the evening and sat at the table nearest the stove with Pitch and Zeke York. Glasses clinked, conversation ebbed and flowed and blue cigar smoke wreathed around the oil lamps. When everyone seemed to be present, Tom Farrow stood up and cleared his throat.

'As your mayor,' he began, 'I want to thank you for comin' out on such a cold night. Now winter's almost done and spring is right around the corner. We're farmin' people here. We know that the best time of year is on its way.'

There was polite applause and calls of, 'too right', and, 'get on with it', from the back of the room. Farrow held up his hand.

'I want to tell you that the best time for Vengeance is on its way too.'

The room fell silent.

'Everybody knows why we're here.

We have a new sheriff. I'm speakin' on behalf of the committee now and I'm tellin' you that we all agree that we have the right man for the job.'

Farrow lowered his voice respectfully.

'Sheriff Parsons was a good man. He stepped up when no one else would. We all knew him and we'll all miss him. But now there's a new era comin' for Vengeance. On behalf of you all, I want to welcome our new sheriff, Mr Eli Pitch.'

Applause and whistles followed. Pitch got to his feet, colour in his cheeks and a self-deprecating grin on his face.

'I want to tell you how good things could be in this town. You all know the Cumberland Mining surveyors have been lookin' at the hills and valleys around here. I'm an independent negotiator and I'm ready to represent you. There ain't nothing Cumberland can throw at me that I can't handle. I want you to know I'm ready for 'em. There's some tough talkin' needs to be done.'

There was a disturbance near the door.

'The Cumberland wants to buy us out,' someone shouted. 'What if we don't want to sell?'

'What matters is prosperity for the town,' Pitch called, 'prosperity for the community and prosperity for us all.'

A woman stood up. Her face was pale and there were dark shadows under her eyes. Her grey hair was pulled back into a bun. She wore a thick blanket round her shoulders over a black dress.

'You all know me. Ma Parsons from the store.'

She looked round at all the different faces.

'Guess I've served every one of you at one time or another. Guess you all know what happened to my late husband too. I know you all reckoned him to be a good man.'

She reached for the back of her chair to support herself.

'What I mean to say is that I know Mr Pitch would have saved my husband if he could. I know he tried. I reckon he's gonna be as good for this town as my Jim was and I want you all to join with me in welcoming Mr Pitch as our new sheriff.'

The crowd applauded as Mrs Parsons sat down. She dabbed her eyes with a cotton handkerchief. Women sitting near her reached over and hugged her.

'I'm humbled, ma'am,' Pitch said. His face twisted into a smile which showed both his sympathy for Mrs Parsons and that he knew how great his responsibility was.

'There's just one thing I'd like you all to know,' Pitch announced.

The applause died again and everyone turned towards him.

'I've made an arrest.'

Silence fell like a stone.

'Me and my associate Mr York were out at the Butterfield place. We had business to discuss with Clay Butterfield. We arrived after dark and the place was empty. Least, we thought it was. Now you all know that Clay and his wife were plannin' on joinin' the wagon train when it comes through. What made him leave early, I don't know. It just seems mighty suspicious to me.'

He paused to let his words hang in the air for a moment.

'Anyhow, the place wasn't empty. The Cajun woman was there and as soon as we announced who we were she started shootin' at us. She didn't stop neither. Fortunately she ain't a good shot, so we're still walkin'.'

'You're talking about Nicolette?' Farrow said. 'Nicolette, who worked here?'

'The wife of the Cajun who shot Sheriff Parsons,' Pitch said.

Ma Parsons cried out and the women hugged her close.

'Then she stole our horses,' Pitch continued. 'We caught up with her heading west out on the open prairie only last night.'

'I told her she didn't ought to set out

on her own,' Sam Logan called from behind the bar. 'She sure was in a mighty hurry to leave and that's a fact.'

'I want to get straight to the point,' Pitch said. 'As your sheriff, I aim to get to the bottom of this. Clay Butterfield running out and now this Cajun running out means something's wrong.'

Conversation filled the saloon like bees. Pitch sat back down. Farrow leaned over to him.

'You got them on your side now.'

Sam began to serve whiskeys at the bar.

Suddenly, the saloon door burst open. Big, square-shouldered Bill Choke stood there.

'Where's the sheriff?' he yelled. 'I've been over to the jailhouse. He's got some crazy woman locked up in there. What are you all doin' in here, anyway?'

Eli Pitch stood up. His tin star gleamed in the lamplight.

'I'm the sheriff.'

Choke looked wildly about the room. 'Where's Jim Parsons?'

Ma Parsons sobbed aloud. Pitch looked Choke in the eye.

'Cajun shot him,' Tom Farrow said. 'Mr Pitch is elected sheriff now.'

Choke took a moment to register this.

'Well you better get up a posse and come damn quick,' Choke said. 'I've just come from John Anderson's place. John and Amy are shot dead and their farm's burned to the ground.'

His words guillotined the noise in the saloon.

'That's right,' he blustered. 'Both of 'em. And I ain't seen no sign of John Junior.'

Shocked silence lasted a minute. Then conversation swarmed again. It grew louder and louder until people were having to shout to be heard. No one knew what to do. The men nearest the bar steadied their nerves with more whiskey; the men nearest the door scanned the street; everyone else talked and argued, proposed theories and made suggestions. Should they remain here all together? Should they return to their homes?

'Now listen up.'

Pitch was on his feet with his arm raised, calling for silence.

'I want a posse of men to ride with me at first light.'

His words broke over the heads of the crowd and inspired them. He stood with his hands planted on his hips, pushing back his jacket to show his silver Colt in its black holster.

'We're gonna ride out and bring in this runaway, Clay Butterfield. Most likely he's lit out west, thinkin' to get ahead of the train.'

Every man in the room was stirred. A posse had never ridden out from Vengeance before. All of them wanted to be in it. They turned, stony faced, to their wives to reassure them. They might be farmers in their daily lives but in their hearts they knew they were gunfighters.

'I want men who can shoot straight and ride fast,' Pitch called above the hubbub. 'I'll take the first ten men who meet me here when dawn breaks.'

The saloon was a hive of noise. Men turned to each other to check who intended to ride and to demand more whiskey from Sam Logan.

'I'm appointing my associate Mr Zachariah York as first deputy,' Pitch called out. 'He's already tasted buckshot out at the Butterfield place. So when we ride out, I'm gonna leave him in charge.'

Zeke allowed Tom Farrow to pin a deputy's star on his jacket. His unsmiling face was pale and glazed with sweat.

'You be sure to leave me the keys to the jailhouse,' he said.

Amazed at what he had started, Bill Choke stood in the doorway of the saloon. Could Clay really have killed John and Amy and burned down their place? What could they have argued about so badly? And this talk of a posse. Everyone knew Clay couldn't shoot. Then Choke imagined a farm which stretched the length of the valley, the Anderson place, the Butterfield place and his own, all joined into one. A farm that belonged to him. So he stood there and listened to the townsfolk convince themselves that Clay Butterfield had killed John and Amy. The more they talked the surer they became.

Bill Choke knew he could have spoken out. He could have urged caution. He could have said that Clay had looked up to John since he was a boy, that they had served in the same unit together, that Clay was heading west because he was a dreamer. He couldn't shoot, he couldn't farm and he had married his crazy cousin. Clay was no good at anything at all. Choke stood aside as men left the saloon to prepare their horses and look out their guns. He did not volunteer for the posse. He said nothing.

Pitch joined him at the bar.

'The town's grateful to you, Mr Choke,' Pitch said. 'You've identified a man who should be brought to justice.'

'I told you about the Anderson farm,' Choke said. 'I never said Clay did it.'

Choke tossed back his whiskey.

'Never said he didn't,' Pitch said.

Choke slammed his glass down on the bar and waved Sam over for a refill.

'Guess you must consider yourself lucky,' Pitch said. 'What happened to Anderson could have happened to you.'

Choke looked at him.

'Why do you say that?'

Pitch shrugged.

'Two miles down the valley ain't far. You ever thought of selling to Cumberland Mining?'

'No,' Choke said. 'Why should I?'

'For a spread like yours, I reckon they'd pay a good price.'

Only a few men were left in the saloon now. Most had gone home intending to be up before dawn and ready to ride. Zeke, still sitting at the table nearest the stove, stretched his injured leg in front of him, leaned back and lit up a stogie. Tom Farrow went behind the bar to supervise Sam washing the glasses.

Pitch moved closer to Choke and lowered his voice.

'You were with the 23rd during the war, weren't you?' Pitch said.

Choke looked surprised at the question.

'So?'

'Ever end up at a place called Campbell's Landing close to Knoxville?'

Pitch leaned back against the bar and surveyed the saloon. The fire in the stove crackled. The air smelt of cigars and sour whiskey.

'Rode all over,' Choke said. 'I try to forget it all now.'

'Forget what you did?'

'It was a terrible time,' Choke said. 'I don't like to think of it.'

He swallowed the last of his whiskey. Pitch watched him.

'Ma Parsons will let me stay at her place,' Choke said. 'They got a room out back of the store.'

He waved a goodnight.

'You ridin' with us in the morning?'

Choke turned in the doorway and shook his head.

'Headin' home,' he said.

Tom Farrow wound down the wicks of the oil lamps and the room fell into darkness. Only a pool of yellow light from the lamp above the bar remained. Sam Logan lined up the clean glasses and waited for Farrow to pay him. Zeke made slow progress on the stairs up to his room. Having pocketed his money, Logan left the saloon and closed the door behind him.

'Peaceful, ain't it?' Farrow said. 'When they've all gone.'

'Time for some shut-eye,' Pitch said. 'We got a few hours.'

Outside, the long main street was silent and lit by the silver moon. The freezing temperature held the air still. A pack of wolves which had gathered on the outskirts of town ventured in. They paraded up the street and darted between the wooden houses. Horses stamped and whinnied as the wolves

surrounded the livery stable, sniffing
and clawing at the edges of the doors.
Then they prowled further until they
passed the last buildings, slipped out
into the shadows of the prairie again
and left the town to sleep.

9

The gang came out of nowhere. They pounded up and down the street firing into the air in a liquor-fueled frenzy. Screams, pistol shots and thundering hoofs burst the stillness of the night. Their torches tore flaming trails in the darkness.

'Any of you Vengeance boys comin' to join us?'

One of them wheeled his horse in the centre of the street, calling out to the houses. Torchlight lit his grinning face.

'Come on now, we got some burnin' to do.'

The men took a few more turns up and down the street.

Eli Pitch tumbled down the saloon stairs, six-gun in hand. Tom Farrow was already at the window covering the street with his scattergun.

'Don't go out there,' Farrow said. 'It

ain't us they're after.'

Pitch stood behind him at the window.

'They'll hightail it in a minute. They just ride in, make a lot of noise, wake everybody up and then they're gone.'

'Know who they are?'

'Regulators. Ain't from around here. They say they want everything back the way it was before the war.'

Pitch watched the men gallop past, their torches flaring.

At the other end of the street, Sam Logan was standing outside the livery stable surrounded by a group of horsemen. He waved his shotgun dangerously.

'You gonna shoot us, old man?'

'Take a step inside my stable and I'll shoot,' Sam said.

He looked desperately up and down the street, expecting help to come running.

One of the men dismounted and walked over to Sam. The barrel of Sam's shotgun wavered.

'I'm warnin' you, mister,' Sam said.

The man grabbed the barrel, pushed it aside and simply lifted the gun out of Sam's hands. He broke open the barrel, let the two cartridges fall to the ground and threw the gun aside. The guys on horseback jeered and catcalled. Sam stood with his arms at his sides while the younger men laughed at him.

'Ain't polite to point guns at folks,' the man said.

He pulled open the stable door.

'These horses look to me like they need some exercise.'

The men on horseback whistled encouragement.

'What are you talking about?' Bewildered, Sam stared into their faces.

The men on horseback covered him with their Colts. One by one, horses emerged from the stable, looked around and trotted along the street.

'We'll chase 'em a mile or two. You can round 'em up in the morning.'

The men wheeled their horses round and with more whoops and laughter, galloped out of town leaving Sam to pick up his shotgun from the mud.

As the first grey streaks of daylight pushed through the darkness, a group of townsmen met at the saloon. Tom Farrow revived the fire in the stove and they all stood round it. The temperature outside was below freezing.

'Why didn't someone come to help me?' Logan said.

'This is a farm town,' Farrow said. 'We don't want no shoot-outs.'

'What about you, Sheriff?' Logan turned to Eli Pitch.

'If you hadn't waved that shotgun in their faces, we wouldn't have to go lookin' for our horses.'

★   ★   ★

Clay built up the fire and put a pot of acorn coffee on to boil. Ice encased the canvas which covered the wagon and frost glittered in the manes of the horses. He stood over the fire until the heat scorched his clothes. Lighting the eastern sky were the first signs of day.

Neither Clay nor Rose Alice had slept much. Rose Alice was tormented by nightmares. She woke with a scream in her mouth and gabbled about fire as Clay held her to him. The darkness grew fears in Clay's mind and he became convinced that Pierre and Nicolette would not follow them and they would always be in danger and alone. Beneath their blankets, he held Rose Alice in his arms as much for his comfort as hers. Then in the hours before dawn the sound of gunshots carried across the frozen prairie from the direction of the town.

Rose Alice climbed down from the wagon to help Clay harness the horses.

'Was I screamin' again?'

'Throwed a scare into the wolf pack. They was gone soon as they heard you.'

Rose Alice pointed at a small carcass roasting on a spit over the fire.

'What's that?'

'Breakfast,' Clay said.

'I ain't hungry.'

'Nor am I,' Clay said. 'Still gonna eat it though.'

'Liar,' Rose Alice said. 'You're always hungry.'

When they finished the harness, they lifted a wooden bench out of the wagon and warmed themselves by the fire. As Clay turned the spit, they watched pale light spread across the sky.

'I never heard you shootin',' Rose Alice said.

'Didn't have to shoot nothin',' Clay said. 'Found 'im right next to the wagon, froze as stiff as a stick.'

Rose Alice shuddered. 'What is it?'

'Good for you,' Clay said. 'That's what it is.'

'Looks like a vole,' Rose Alice said distastefully.

Clay fetched some hard tack from the wagon and divided the meat in half. It came to barely a mouthful each.

'Think Nicolette will come today?' Rose Alice said.

'Can't say,' Clay said. His night time fears were still with him.

He put his arm round Rose Alice's shoulders and drew her closer to the fire. The sun brought daylight but no warmth.

'I was thinkin' of riding back,' Clay said.

Rose Alice moved away from him. She fumbled inside the blanket that was wrapped round her shoulders and pulled out her piece of embroidered cloth and pressed it to her cheek.

'Why? All we got to do is wait for Pierre and Nicolette. Then Pierre can ride back and get the hundred dollars. You said so yourself.'

'It ain't the hundred dollars,' Clay said.

'What is it then? You think Pierre and Nicolette ain't gonna come?'

'No.'

Clay looked at her frightened face.

'What if Zeke and this other guy follow us?' he said.

Rose Alice rearranged the linen so the flowers hung round her neck like a garland. She stared into the fire.

'If he's done that to John Anderson, maybe he'll follow us out here.'

'We'll be far away,' Rose Alice said. 'He'll never catch us. That's what you said.'

'If he rode out from town, he could,' Clay said.

'We better keep running,' Rose Alice said. 'We got to go right now. I don't want you leaving me out here, Clay.'

She moved the linen against her cheek again.

'Anyhow, if you ride back into town,' Rose Alice continued, 'what can you do?'

Clay looked at her.

'I got to stop him,' he said. 'I got to be sure he ain't never gonna come after us.'

★   ★   ★

Four prairie schooners sailed into Vengeance at midday. Three were hauled by two pairs and one was smaller and drawn by only one. The three larger wagons were owned by tenant farmers from northern Tennessee whose lives had not recovered from the war. Pierre's brother Roy Calcasieu and his wife Martine owned the smaller wagon. Pierre and Nicolette had agreed to wait for them at Independence, Missouri where they would join a larger train and head out together along the Oregon Trail.

The wagons lined up at the western end of Main Street opposite the livery stable. Ragged children tumbled out, delighted to find buildings rather than the usual grassy wilderness to explore at the end of a journey. The women folk climbed down and headed for the store in search of news about life in town. The men inspected the wagons and checked the horses. They noticed the saloon, but for the moment resisted temptation and crossed the street to the livery stable to inquire about the prices.

'Pierre must have been through here,' Roy said. 'I wish he'd have waited for us.' The men from the wagons were surprised to find the livery stable empty and unattended. They wandered down the street towards the saloon.

'Ain't no one around,' one of them called to Roy.

Roy and Martine strolled down the street. Vengeance seemed much like the other farm towns they had passed. They held the vision of a new built house and rolling acres in California in their hearts and there was nothing here which would induce them to stay. They also knew that being Arcadians they would always be outsiders in a place like this. The people on the train were pleasant enough to their faces, but they both knew that they had to be twice as welcoming and be seen to work twice as hard to earn their respect. California could not come quick enough.

Sam Logan trotted his horse down the street. He was riding bareback and led a second horse by a rope. He nodded politely to Roy and Martine as he passed and turned towards the stable. They followed him.

'Regulators,' Logan explained. 'Busted in here last night and set all the horses loose. Everyone is outa town lookin' for 'em.'

'Ever met a man called Pierre Calcasieu?' Roy said. 'Must have come through here before winter.'

'I liked him,' Sam said. 'Everyone did.'

Sam dismounted and led the horses into the stable.

'But then,' he added, 'what can you expect?'

Sam busied himself with finding hay for the horses.

'Expect what?' Roy said.

'You a relative of his?' Sam said. 'You talk like he did.'

Roy clutched Martine's arm and held it tight.

'Brother,' Roy said.

'He taught me some of that Cajun talk,' Sam said. '*Mon cher*, ain't it?'

Sam picked up a hay fork.

'Bad blood came through in the end,' Sam continued. 'Bein' from down that way, guess he couldn't help it.'

Sam looked at Roy and Martine.

'Don't you know?' he said.

Neither of them answered.

'Got caught cheating at cards,' Sam said. 'Got shot.'

Sam began to turn the hay pile.

'Who shot him?'

'Sheriff.'

Sam concentrated on the hay, shaking it loose from his fork and watching it fall.

''Course,' Sam said. 'He wasn't sheriff then.'

'Nicolette?' Martine said.

'She was real nice too. Known for bein' a hard worker.'

'She's dead too?'

'In jail,' Sam said. 'She took to shootin' at the sheriff. Then she took off in her wagon in the middle of the night. I told her not to, but she sure wanted to get out of town fast. Sheriff rode out after her.'

The only sound was the swish of hay falling from Sam's fork.

'I'm real sorry,' Sam said. 'Musta been bad blood comin' through. Else why would they have done them things? I reckon they couldn't help themselves.'

Martine pulled Roy towards the door.

'Got plenty of hay,' Sam called. 'If you need some for your horses.'

Outside, the light was bright after the shadows of the stable. The timber buildings were bleached by sun and rain and the street was dark with mud, though an inch or two below the surface the ground was frozen. The men from the wagons had gone to the saloon and the women were still at the store.

'There's the sheriff's office, right there.'

Roy pointed a few yards down the street. Martine grasped his arm.

'Be careful,' she said. 'You know what they think of us.'

Roy pushed open the door. A man with a star pinned to his jacket sat behind a desk. His leg was stretched out and supported by a chair. He had a matchstick clenched between his teeth. A pair of Colts, a dirty rag and a small can of oil were on the desk in front of him. The chambers were empty and the shells were upright in two rows of six. A gunbelt with empty holsters hung by the door. On the wall, there was a rifle rack with two Winchesters and four spaces. On the opposite side of the room were the steel bars of a single cell. Behind the bars, Nicolette sat on a bench.

Nicolette jumped up when Roy entered and put her hand over her mouth to stop herself from crying out. The man behind the desk looked startled and collapsed the lines of shells with a sweep of his hand.

'Sheriff?' Roy said.

'Who wants to know?' Zeke said.

'Roy Calcasieu. Just come in on a wagon.'

Zeke's eyes narrowed.

'You another Cajun?'

Roy smiled pleasantly.

'Heading for California,' Roy said. 'Join a train at Independence.'

Zeke removed the matchstick from his mouth and inspected the chewed end.

'What do you want?'

'How much is her bail?' Roy said.

He nodded towards Nicolette.

Zeke replaced the matchstick and used his tongue to move it to the side of his mouth.

'How much you got?'

'I asked how much the bail was,' Roy said.

Zeke laughed.

'I'm the deputy,' Zeke said. 'Sheriff's out of town.'

Roy looked Zeke in the eye.

'You can fix bail, can't you?'

'I can,' Zeke said. 'But sheriff's took the keys with him. Reckon he don't want me getting the other side of that cell door, since this one scattered our horses and I had to walk every which way on my bad leg to get 'em back.'

'When do you expect the sheriff back?' Roy said.

Zeke laughed.

'When he comes.'

10

'I know you're scared,' Clay said. 'But that's all it is. Being scared ain't gonna hurt you.'

Clay swung himself up into the saddle and looked down at Rose Alice. Her blanched face peeped out from under a swathe of blankets, the embroidered linen was tight around her neck and her thumb was in her mouth. Her other hand hung down at her side and held a hatchet.

'I left you the shotgun,' Clay said. 'There's plenty of shells. Just remember to hold it tight into your shoulder like I told you. Build up a big fire tonight, as big as you can. Tether your horse round the same side of the wagon the fire is. Then if the wolves come, they'll leave you alone.'

Clay couldn't think of any more advice to give her.

Rose Alice stared at him.

'I'm comin' back,' Clay said. 'I promise. A day or two ain't long.'

She took her thumb out of her mouth.

'I don't want you to go.'

'You make me nervous when you say that, Rose Alice. I just know that if these fellas done that to the Andersons, they ain't gonna let us get away.'

Clay looked away from her, back towards the town, as if to check that there was no one coming.

'We were gettin' away. We were runnin',' Rose Alice persisted.

Clay shook his head.

'If they come after us and something happens, I'd think I could have stopped them and I didn't even try.'

Rose Alice slipped her thumb back in her mouth and stared at Clay with haunted eyes.

'Don't you try to stop me, Rose Alice, I'm scared enough for the two of us as it is.'

Clay turned his horse towards town.

Rose Alice watched him ride until he was a speck on the horizon. The cold morning air cut through her blankets and she realized the fire had died.

Rose Alice began to sort through the pile of kindling Clay had left for her. She made a spark, blew on it and watched the flame catch on the bark shavings Clay had made with his knife. When they were in the cabin, Clay always made the fire, she reflected. Sometimes it took him forever and she sat there while the cold gnawed her bones, but he always did it in the end. He used to tell her that when they got to California, they wouldn't need a fire except for cooking; they wouldn't need blankets on the beds, only cotton sheets because it would be summer all year round. She smiled to herself at the idea of it, the things he said just to make her laugh.

The fire was strong now. Rose Alice sat close and felt the warmth on her legs. She threw on some of the larger sticks Clay had left for her. With her thumb slipped into her mouth, her other hand holding the hatchet, she became mesmerized by the flames. There were horsemen in there and she watched them gallop right up to her and then turn and ride far away. There were faces. Sometimes they were twisted, wicked faces laughing at her and trying to scare her. At other times they were people she knew. Or had known. It was a strange pleasure to see them again and she kept staring because she knew that if she looked away from the fire they would disappear because they only lived in the fire now.

Rose Alice saw her mother and father and felt a great surge of joy that they should be there. They were just standing there just like they had stood in an old photograph she used to have, her father standing tall behind her mother with his hand resting on her shoulder, staring straight into the camera. And her mother seated beside him with her hands folded neatly in her lap, her sweet smile playing at her lips, wearing her prettiest dress.

Her younger brothers and sisters were there too, all laughing and playing like they used to. And Rose Alice was so happy to see them, she could almost hear them calling her name. Then she realized that they were. They were calling her name. Not calling. Shouting. Screaming her name out loud, again and again. Screaming for her to save them from the flames. And her mother and father were there too in the burning house. Somehow it was too late for them because there was blood on their faces and they were already dead.

But Rose Alice couldn't get to her brothers and sisters because of the horsemen. One of them was dismounting now. He had dismounted and he was striding towards her. She backed into the wood shed where her father stacked all the split logs so neatly and she could see the horseman laughing as he made a grab for her, so she reached behind her and there was a hatchet in her hand and she swung it at him again and again. And he was laughing because he kept ducking backwards, making her hack the empty air.

Then she saw that he was steadying himself on the edge of the woodpile with his left hand. She swung the hatchet and felt it bite into the logs. She wrenched it free so she could swing at him again and she saw that he was holding up his hand and there was blood pouring down his wrist and he was screaming now because two of his fingers were missing. He tumbled out into the yard. She followed him ready to swing at him again.

The house was blazing, its flames rearing into the night sky. One end of the barn was on fire. Mounted men were there in grey uniforms. They pulled him up into the saddle. She saw one of them draw his gun and she ran towards the barn. She heard the bullet ricochet off the edge of the door. She ducked back into the shadows expecting him to follow her. But he didn't. She heard the shouts of the men and the hoof beats as they galloped out of the yard.

Rose Alice could smell burning. She was standing too close to the fire. Flames were singeing a corner of the blanket she had draped over her. The hatchet was in her hand. She examined the blade, expecting to see blood but there was none. She stepped back into the cold morning air. Clay was gone and she was alone on the prairie.

* * *

As the afternoon wore on, men began to drift back into town. Some came on foot leading two or three horses, others rode bareback. Roy sat on the seat of his wagon checking each man who passed to see if he was wearing a sheriff's star. Eventually, Pitch trotted down the street towards the stables on a black mare. He glared at Roy and the other people from the wagons as he rode past.

Roy let Pitch stable his horse and

then followed him into the sheriff's office. Zeke was still sitting there with his leg propped on a chair. Nicolette was still behind bars.

Pitch jerked his thumb at Zeke to show he wanted his seat.

'This fella came in earlier.' Zeke nodded at Roy. 'Wanted to pay bail for the Cajun.'

Pitch flicked back the side of his jacket to show his silver Colt. Zeke struggled to his feet and gasped as he put weight on his leg.

'Still got buckshot in my leg,' he said. 'Could have got her to take it out if you'd left the keys.'

Pitch sat down, took his six-gun from its holster and laid it on the desk in front of him. He looked up at Roy, stony faced.

Roy repeated his question about the price of Nicolette's bail. Pitch sized him up. Poor clothes, no gun: another farmer, a guy who has spent everything he has on a wagon to chase some dream in the west. A guy whose wife and children, if he has any, are destined for a prairie grave.

'There ain't no bond,' Pitch said.

Zeke leaned against the door.

'You gonna just keep her here?'

'I'm waitin' on someone to come in to pay,' Pitch said.

'I'm here. I'll pay,' Roy said.

'Price is the deeds to a farm,' Pitch said.

Roy looked over at Nicolette. Outside the windows, the sky was darkening.

'Let me make you an offer,' Roy said.

Pitch picked up his Colt and pointed it at Roy's chest.

'Who were you with in the war?' Pitch said.

'Wasn't with no one,' Roy said. 'Arrived in New Orleans the year the war ended.'

Pitch nodded. He lowered the pistol.

'When are these wagons rolling out?'

'Tomorrow,' Roy said. 'But I ain't leaving without her.'

'You hungry?' Pitch called over to Nicolette.

Nicolette turned away and refused to look at him.

'If you want to do something for her, bring her some food,' Pitch said.

When Roy had gone, Zeke said, 'Unlock that door and let her finish taking the shot out of my leg. It's been burning me up all day.'

'You could get Tom Farrow to do it,' Pitch suggested.

'Have you seen the way he carves a chicken?' Zeke said.

Pitch unclipped a set of keys from his belt and unlocked the cell door. Zeke sat with his leg up on the chair again. He put a canteen of water on the desk and wiped his Bowie on his shirt tail. Pitch reached into a desk drawer and brought out a half empty bottle of red-eye. Zeke grimaced as he peeled away layers of cotton bandage which were stiff with dried blood.

'Why should I help you?' Nicolette glared at Zeke.

Pitch grabbed her by the wrist and hauled her out into the room. He picked up his gun and jabbed her in the ribs. There was a metallic snick as he eased back the hammer with his thumb.

'I'm keeping you here until your friend Clay Butterfield turns up. The deeds to that run down farm of his is what's gonna get you out of jail. So until he comes, you do what I say.'

Nicolette picked up the Bowie and inspected the wound. Amidst the ripped skin and torn muscle there were four black specks.

'Got to get the shot out now,' she said. 'Before it works its way further in.'

She freed the cork from the whiskey bottle with her teeth and splashed the wound. Then she took a slug herself. As she prodded the wound with the tip of the knife, Zeke gripped the sides of the chair until his knuckles cracked. Eventually, four pieces of shot clattered on to the floor and she doused the wound with whiskey again. She looked up at Pitch.

'Clay ain't comin',' she said. 'He's run out on me. There ain't no point in you holding me now.'

'If he ain't here by morning I'll ride out and bring him in myself,' Pitch said.

Nicolette looked at Zeke.

'Pull out that shirt tail.'

She picked up the Bowie again and cut off strips of cotton.

'What have you got against Clay anyway?' Nicolette continued. 'He's just a farmer like the others. Only he ain't no good at it.'

Pitch glowered at her.

'He was in the 23rd.'

Zeke grimaced as Nicolette tightened the strips of cotton round his leg. She lifted the oil lamp off the desk so the pool of light shone on the bandage and allowed her to inspect her work. Spots of blood already showed through.

'So what if he was?' Nicolette said.

Pitch's face was in shadow.

'They burned my house. My family was inside.'

Zeke was breathing in short gasps.

He gripped the edge of the chair again as the pain bit.

'Was they hell,' Zeke said. 'When they burned the house, your folks was long gone. There weren't no bodies.'

'That's a lie,' Pitch roared. 'The Yankees burned 'em in their beds. They didn't have a chance. I lost everything that day.'

He grabbed Nicolette by the hair and towed her back into the cell and threw her inside.

'The 23rd done it. They was all there: that fool sheriff, Anderson, Butterfield, Choke. I got their regimental list. They took everything I had. Burned the house, the barns, torched the woods and the fields, killed everyone. My wife would never run out on me.'

Pitch turned the key in the lock.

The office door swung open and Martine stood there holding a tray of food.

'That ain't how I remember it,' Zeke said.

The whole valley, a single farm. Bill Choke felt the blood surge in his veins. He had never dared dream of anything like this. Of course, some men risked everything and headed west on the wagon trains. But those were men with nothing to lose. Who else would drag their wives and ragged children two thousand miles for the chance things might turn out better? They weren't like him. He would be wealthy now if the war hadn't come.

But the chance of owning the whole valley. Choke didn't have to go to California. California had come to him. As he rode, he began dividing up the valley in his mind. The extra land would mean increased collateral at the bank. He would be able to hire men to clear the woods for arable land. He would sell the timber, buy breeding mares and breed horses. Why shouldn't he start a herd of beeves? This wasn't cattle country but the grass was good here and the market for beef was rising year on year. Or sheep. The valley was big enough. If the high ground at the eastern end was cleared, he could keep sheep there in the summer and bring them down into pens in the winter.

With all these plans filling his head, Choke was excited to be heading home. He wanted to be back at the kitchen table with pen and paper in hand so he could translate his thoughts into figures and read back his own cash projections. He was glad to be out of the town in any event. He puzzled over the way the new sheriff had asked him about the war. He had seemed to know which regiment Choke had been in even though he had never set eyes on him before.

Choke couldn't abide the town now. It had grown since his father's time as the land round about was divided up into farms. When he was a boy, the Parsons family arrived and set up the store. He could recall the day the saloon opened and had watched the livery stable being built. It had been a sleepy, neighbourly place then where everyone knew everyone else. For years, no one thought of appointing a sheriff. Then Tom Farrow had announced that the town should have a mayor and because he put himself forward for the post, everyone agreed that he should take it on. Then Farrow decided that as mayor, he would appoint a sheriff. Flattered to be asked and because there were no real duties to perform, old Jim Parsons agreed to do it.

In Bill Choke's opinion, since the war Vengeance had gone to the dogs. Regulators rode through and caused trouble, wagons had started arriving from the south on their way to Missouri bringing all manner of undesirables. There were even a couple of Arcadians who had lived in their wagon right on main street all winter. On top of that, the prices in the saloon had never been higher. Choke only went in to town to pick up supplies now and always left as soon as he could.

At midday, the sun was still pale but

the air had warmed slightly. Choke reached the top of a ridge which gave him a good view of the landscape. The western end of the valley snaked here so the town was hidden in one direction and the woods above his own farm were hidden in the other. Below him and to the west he could make out the roof of Clay Butterfield's cabin hidden amongst a stand of tulip poplars. He hadn't been down there for years, but knowing Clay, the roof would be leaking and the walls would be damp. He began to calculate how much it would cost for a couple of men to demolish it, fell the poplars and haul the timber into town to be sold. They could complete the job in a week, ten days at the outside.

To Bill Choke's right, a group of black vultures was gathered at the foot of a hackberry, gorging themselves on some carcass. Disgusting creatures. Choke had seen what they could do to a live piglet. Instinctively, he flapped his arms and shouted at them. The birds hopped a few paces away and stared at him. Choke wasn't interested in the carcass they had been attacking, but as he looked away, something caught his eye. He peered at it and turned his horse off the track to take a look. The birds retreated a few more paces. He could see it clearly now. It was a boot.

The eyes had been pecked out of the skull, the cheeks and tongue had been torn away. The clothing was tattered, blood soaked and ripped from the body. The torso was gouged open and gutted. Half eaten internal organs were strewn across the ground. The vultures studied Choke from a few yards away.

Choke knew who it was by the jacket. It was John Anderson Junior's, he had seen him wear it a hundred times. It was his father's old hunting jacket. The pockets sagged where they had once held shotgun shells; the lapels were picked away by fishing hooks. The coarse weave was soaked with blood. Choke drew his Colt and fired at the group of vultures. The birds screeched, flapped their huge wings and blundered up into the air.

The vultures wouldn't have attacked the boy while he was alive, would they? Had he been heading for town and died from the cold? You could see the Butterfield place from here. Had Clay lost his mind and come after him, hell bent on wiping out the whole family? Maybe John Junior had witnessed what had happened back at his farm and been heading for town to fetch help when Clay caught up with him, shot him and left him as carrion. That must be it. John Junior had seen Clay murder his parents.

Bill Choke knew that the decent thing to do would be to ride back into town and find an undertaker. He considered this for a moment. What would be the point? Even if one of the townsfolk arranged a funeral, John Junior had no family to stand at his graveside now. Distasteful as it seemed, maybe it was best to let the vultures do their work. Someone would come

174

across the body when the bones had been picked clean.

Sickened to his stomach, Choke turned his horse back to the road. He wanted to get away from the mutilated corpse and get home. He urged his horse on. As he rode through the grey afternoon light, he reflected that now the valley was as good as his. He may have to wait before he could annex the Anderson place as the new sheriff was bound to make some sort of investigation into the deaths. But Clay and his wife had deserted their property. What was to stop him claiming it right away? Maybe tomorrow he would ride over to the Butterfield place and make a start on tearing down the cabin.

11

At midday, Clay first noticed the inverted 'U' shape of a covered wagon on the horizon. He assumed it was moving but later realized he was wrong. Then he saw that there was no smoke and that puzzled him. No one stopped on the plains without lighting a fire. As he drew closer he saw that the horses were gone. Who would abandon a wagon out here? When he was within a hundred yards, he realized the wagon belonged to Pierre and Nicolette. Clay called out his friends' names as he approached but knew there would be no answer. He dismounted and climbed aboard.

At first glance, everything seemed in order. The mountain of furniture was secured with ropes, the bedding was folded, the wooden chest which held the supplies was untouched and the keg of drinking water was full. There was a tear in the canvas over his head. This was unusual because Pierre was scrupulous about repairs. Maybe he hadn't noticed it. They had probably done it loading the furniture.

Hungry as he was, Clay resisted the temptation of helping himself to a handful of Nicolette's hard tack. He climbed over the back board of the wagon and scanned the horizon. No one. Then he noticed the bullets embedded in the tailboard. His heart froze. He walked round the wagon expecting to find bodies in the mud. He made a second circuit, wider this time. Then another.

Pierre had realized Clay and Rose Alice had headed out and come looking for them, just as Clay knew he would. Why would he have abandoned everything and gone back to town? Clay inspected the wagon and the ground around it, looking for signs of blood. Somehow it would make more sense if he found bloodstains. But there were none. He checked that the canvas awning was secure, remounted and continued on towards town. He would be there after dark. Away to the east, black vultures circled like specks of dirt in the sky.

Clay still hadn't figured out what this stranger wanted with him. He'd been over and over everything he could remember about what happened down around Knoxville. But there had been so much devastation. One burning town after another, farm after devastated farm. And the bodies. You expected to see them after the battles. Clay remembered watching the burial detail after Perryville, the groups of black soldiers picking their way over the ruined landscape, stretchering the anonymous dead to mass graves. Then you came across the victims of forgotten skirmishes at the roadside, sprawled on the floors of burned out houses or rotting in barns.

There was nothing Clay had done which could cause someone to come after him and nothing his unit had done which was worse than any other. Clay was certain of it. His Colt was strapped to his hip, he was determined to settle this. His new life in the west was waiting for him.

It had been dark for two hours when Clay reached the edge of town. The temperature had fallen and a film of ice had formed on the mud underfoot. The yellow glow of oil lamps filled some of the windows on main street and there were torches burning in their iron racks on each side of the saloon door. The sky glittered with stars, cold moonlight shone on the buildings and the line of wagons while shadows filled the unlit spaces.

Clay took his horse to the stable. Sam Logan waved a shotgun in his face as soon as he pushed open the door.

'Been sleeping right here behind the door,' he said. 'They ain't getting away with it a second time.'

He told Clay about the Regulators and the day they'd all spent searching for their horses.

'New sheriff wasn't no use,' Logan continued. 'I could have got killed and he didn't even show his face.'

It took Clay a while before he realized Sam wasn't talking about Sheriff Parsons.

'You better come out back,' Sam said. 'There's been changes.'

The two men sat by Sam's fire at the back of the stable while he told Clay how Pierre had shot Sheriff Parsons, about the election of Eli Pitch and how Nicolette was locked in jail. Clay was silent. 'There's a fella in town who wants to kill you,' Zeke had said.

'I liked Pierre and Nicolette. I truly did,' Sam said. 'Even if they were Cajuns. They had their wagon parked right beside the stable all winter, insisted on payin' me for it too.'

Sam took a swig of his coffee.

'Bad blood,' he said. 'They say it always comes through in the end.'

Clay threw his coffee grounds into the fire. Steam hissed.

'That's bull,' Clay said. 'All blood's the same colour. Where will the sheriff be now?'

'In the saloon. Seems to me him and Tom Farrow are plannin' to run the town between them.'

Clay stood up.

'Don't you tell no one I was here,' Clay said.

The sheriff's office was in darkness when Clay slipped in through the unlocked door. Alarmed by the silhouette of a man sneaking in and assuming Zeke had persuaded the sheriff to let him have the keys, Nicolette backed into the corner of the cell and clenched her fists.

'It's me,' Clay said.

Nicolette sobbed with relief. Clay searched every drawer and ran his hand over every peg in the office, hoping to find a spare set of keys.

'Looks like you're gonna have to wait a while,' Clay said.

Nicolette told him to go to Roy and Martine's wagon.

'They're good people,' she said. 'They'll hide you.'

Out on the street, Clay looked at the torches flaring on each side of the saloon door. He could walk in there right now. He had his gun. He knew how to use it. You can't hit a rabbit with a scattergun. How are you gonna face down a gunfighter in a saloon? The cold bit through his jacket and he remembered he hadn't eaten for hours. He thought of Rose Alice, alone out on the prairie and how he had to get back to her. He remembered their cabin, how the fire crackled and how the orange light made the shadows dance.

The scraping sound of the stable door opening echoed through the darkness. From the back of Roy's wagon, Clay watched a lone horseman ride out into the night. He trotted the length of the street and headed east out of town. Clay waited but no one followed. He watched Sam pull the stable door closed. Roy and Martine gave him food and blankets and made a space for him to sleep. Nicolette was right: they were good people.

*　*　*

Zeke stood on the porch of Bill Choke's place at first light. Choke had watched him approach from the safety of the house.

'What do you want?' Choke called through the locked door.

'I want to talk business with you, Mr Choke,' Zeke said. 'Got a proposition.'

'At this hour?' Choke said.

But he could not resist. The bolts on the door rattled back and Choke waved Zeke inside. He covered him with his handgun, but put it down as soon as he saw Zeke was not holding a weapon.

The room was furnished with a table, hard chairs and a couch with blankets untidily strewn across it. On the table, an oil lamp stood beside a ledger open at a page showing columns of figures. There was a pile of logs beside the fireplace in which the embers of last night's fire still glowed. Someone was moving about in a kitchen which adjoined the room. There was the warm smell of baking bread. Choke called out to his wife to bring coffee. He snapped his ledger shut and gestured Zeke to sit at the table while he lit the lamp and built up the fire.

'You're the new deputy, ain't you?' Choke said. 'Businessman as well as a lawman.' He chuckled to himself.

'Zachariah York,' Zeke said.

He looked towards the open kitchen door and then back at Choke. He lowered his voice to a whisper.

'There's someone in town who aims to kill you.'

Colour drained from Choke's face. He shoved his chair back from the table.

'You rode out here to threaten me?'

'No,' Zeke said. 'I got a proposition for you.'

'Who would want to kill me?'

'Eli Pitch.'

'The new sheriff?'

Choke recalled Clay Butterfield standing beside him the day his bag was stuffed with quail saying something about a list of names. The sheriff had known he'd ridden with the 23rd.

'Why?'

Ellen Choke came in from the kitchen carrying a pot of coffee and two cups. She glanced anxiously at Zeke, set the cups down on the table and filled them.

'Fire stayed in all night?' she said.

'Yes,' Choke said.

Ellen Choke scanned the room, looking for anything amiss. She crossed the room to the mantelpiece, picked up a key and wound the clock which sat above the fire place. Then she gathered up the heap of blankets from the couch and took them with her.

Choke waited until she had left the room.

'You're saying the sheriff wants to kill me?'

Zeke nodded.

'Everyone in the 23rd. He says they

set fire to his house outside of Campbell's Landing with his wife and children still inside.'

Choke stood up, picked up the ledger and set it down on the couch.

'Ridiculous,' Choke said.

'I know who burned that house and it weren't the 23rd,' Zeke said.

Choke started to pace up and down in front of the fire. Five paces up, five paces back.

'He aims to kill all of you and take everything you own,' Zeke said.

Choke stopped still and looked at him.

'Is that what this is about?'

'Look at it how you want,' Zeke said. 'He's already got the deeds to the Anderson place.'

'What?'

Choke looked out of the window. In his mind's eye, he saw a farm which ran the length of the valley. Then he saw John Anderson's body half covered with burned timbers. He began pacing again.

'He did that to John?'

Choke sat down at the table again.

'Pretty soon the whole town will blame Butterfield,' Zeke said. 'If they ain't already.'

Choke placed his hands on the table in front of him and laced and unlaced his fingers.

'Cumberland Mining will pay top price for land at this end of the valley,' Zeke added.

'This is farming country,' Choke said. 'I threw those surveyors off my land.'

'Open cast,' Zeke said. 'Top price.'

'What's your point?' Choke said.

'You pay me and I'll kill him for you.'

Choke laughed.

'You're his deputy.'

'He ain't gonna suspect me. Next time he sees you you're a dead man.'

Ellen Choke stood in the kitchen doorway. She held the percolator in her hand and the lid rattled.

'You gentlemen like me to freshen that coffee?'

Choke waved her away.

Zeke nodded towards the kitchen door, leaned across the table and lowered his voice.

'It won't just be you.'

'How much?' Choke said.

'A thousand dollars.'

Choke glared at him.

'If I kill him myself, it'll cost me the price of a bullet.'

'You kill the sheriff, you'll have the whole town after you. I do it and no one will ever see me again.'

Outside the window, the day brightened. Sunlight showed through the clouds and frost was beginning to fade from the fields. The men heard the clang of the oven door from the kitchen. The smell of baking was strong now.

'He's your partner,' Choke said.

'We've rode a long way together,' Zeke agreed. 'Now he's aiming to cut me out. Farrow made him sheriff and he'll want payback. Eli ain't one to divide things more than two ways. I

heard 'em talking. There'll be a killing
and they'll find a way of pinning it on
me.' Zeke laughed. 'Could even be
yours.'

Choke's face was stone.

'You say you'll ride out the same day
you do it?'

Zeke nodded.

'I ain't got a thousand dollars,'
Choke said. 'I can give you two
hundred right now.'

'Ain't enough,' Zeke said. 'You got
money in the bank?'

'Some,' Choke said.

'Then you better give me the two
hundred and get to the bank without
him seeing you,' Zeke said. 'Reckon
he'll be riding out after Butterfield
today.'

'Two hundred now and four hundred
more,' Choke said.

Zeke stared at him.

'Five hundred more.'

12

Lack of sleep made Rose Alice jumpy. Huddled under all the blankets they owned, she crouched in the back of the wagon with the shotgun across her knees. As she stared out over the silver prairie, she heard wolves howl and watched an owl swoop on a prairie mouse and fly off into the night. A grey fox came close to the wagon but ran off into the darkness when she banged the shotgun against the wooden side. She was doing a good job: the goat and the chickens were safe.

Before dawn, a freezing wind got up. Rose Alice drew the blankets tight. Fear for Clay's safety spidered across her brain. When he told her he intended to ride back into town, she hadn't known whether to feel proud or angry. He had never left her for more than a day before. And where was Nicolette? She missed Nicolette so much, the excited way she talked, her musical laughter whenever they mentioned California.

As the wind moved clouds across the moon, the prairie fell into darkness. The canvas sides of the wagon flapped, the goat shifted in her sleep and the embers of the dying fire brightened as the wind passed over. Rose Alice imagined noises: a scratching underneath the wagon, as if a wolf was trying to gnaw his way in; a scraping at the canvass roof, as if some giant bird of prey had landed on it. She could hear the noises quite clearly even though her head was filled with the moan of the wind. Her hand tightened on the stock of the shotgun and her finger was ready on the trigger.

The sounds came and went. The fire glowed and faded. The wind's lament was sometimes close, sometimes far away. In the darkness, Rose Alice felt for the coarse hair of the goat's back and for the sticks which were the bars of the chickens' cage to remind herself that she had protected them. She had kept them safe.

As the sky began to lighten, the wind dropped. Rose Alice climbed down out of the wagon and rebuilt the fire. The air was sharp against her face and the cold knifed through her clothes. She let down the tailboard of the wagon, allowed the goat to jump out and tethered her to a wheel. She stood the coffee pot at the edge of the fire while she checked on the horse.

As Rose Alice passed the end of the wagon she saw that there was an egg in one of the chicken cages. She reached in for it and loved the feel of its warmth and perfect smoothness in her hand. She was surprised to realize that she was hungry. Usually the thought of food made her feel sick, but this morning it was different. She slid the egg into the coffee pot and watched as the lid clattered and steam puffed from the spout.

Rose Alice knew what she was going to do. She decided in an instant without even thinking about it. The wolves wouldn't come in daylight, especially if she built up the fire. The chickens were safe in their cages. The only one who was in danger now was Clay. She had to be with him. If he was on his way back, she would meet him, if not she would have the shotgun with her.

Breakfast warmed her and the success of her night's work made her strong. Rose Alice reached underneath the blanket and pulled off her embroidered scarf. She ran her fingers over the silk flowers which she loved so much; she had watched her mother sew every stitch. She folded it neatly, smoothed it flat with the palm of her hand and tucked it behind the tailboard of the wagon. She picked up the shotgun and climbed up on to the horse. She didn't know how far the town was, but she had seen the direction Clay took the previous day. That was enough. As she rode away from the wagon, the morning began to brighten.

'Look at this.'

Farrow burst through the saloon doors and held a letter out to Eli Pitch who was in his usual place at the table nearest the stove.

'Just opened it. Came in on the stage from Frankfort.'

Pitch took the paper, noted the Cumberland Mining Company of Kentucky letterhead and scanned the rest of the page.

'Pulling out?'

'That's what it says,' Farrow said.

Pitch read aloud: 'After costly delays caused by landowners along the valley east of Vengeance, the board of directors have unanimously decided to abandon all attempts to seek permission for test drilling in the area.'

He looked up.

'What delays?'

'Read on,' Farrow said.

'The landowners have either failed to answer written communication from us or have expressed outright hostility when our surveyors visited them in person. The directors now consider that further delay would be detrimental to the prosperity of the company . . . '

'What about our prosperity?' Farrow blustered. 'They don't say nothing about that.'

' . . . And have decided to explore the possibility of exploiting mineral wealth elsewhere in our great state.'

Pitch threw the letter down on the table.

'I'm hungry. I've been sitting here waiting for breakfast.'

'Well, you're gonna have to wait some more,' Farrow snapped. 'The cook's sick, there's only me here and I've been over at the store.'

'Bring me coffee and breakfast and let me think,' Pitch said.

A group of local men wandered in from the street and sat down at a table. Pitch recognized them from the night of his election. They called out a 'mornin', Sheriff' to him. Pitch glowered.

Farrow returned with Pitch's coffee.

'Come on, Tom,' one of the men called. 'Ain't just the sheriff needs coffee in the morning.'

'I'm shorthanded,' Farrow snapped.

'Where's that Cajun girl?' the man said. 'The one that was always smiling.'

'I'll bring your coffee,' Farrow said. 'You all want breakfast?'

Farrow disappeared into the kitchen.

The men started to grumble about the time breakfast was taking. One of them took out a pack of cards and began to shuffle.

Farrow came out of the kitchen and whispered in Pitch's ear.

'Let me have Nicolette back just for the morning otherwise nobody ain't gonna get fed. You can lock her back up again after that.'

'Tommy,' one of the men called. 'You ain't brought us no coffee.'

'You and me need time to talk,' Pitch hissed. 'If the girl runs off, you can run after her.'

Pitch swigged back the rest of his

coffee. On his way over to the sheriff's office, he passed people from the wagons heading towards the saloon. Clay watched from inside Roy and Martine's wagon. He saw the sheriff enter his office, leave a couple of minutes later and frogmarch Nicolette towards the saloon.

Clay felt his good intentions waver. Back in his wagon, everything had seemed clear cut. He knew what he had to do: just ride into town and confront the sheriff. He had to make sure he could leave for California and his new life without being followed. But now, with Nicolette in jail, her wagon abandoned and Pierre killed, everything was different. The sheriff had tried to get up a posse to come looking for him once. If they rode out now they would find Rose Alice. Staying here, he put Roy and Martine in danger.

Someone left the store further up the street. Clay jumped down from the back of the wagon and turned towards a doorway to hide his face. Whoever it was headed off in the opposite direction and failed to notice him. Hugging the storefronts, Clay continued up the street. People passed him, on their way to breakfast at the saloon. He glanced in at the window of the sheriff's office. It was empty. The chair was pushed back from the desk and the cell door was open with its key in the lock. Clay felt sweat prick the back of his neck. He glanced up and down the street, ducked inside the office, grabbed the cell key and was out on the street inside a minute.

A group of women standing outside Ma Parsons' store were looking in Clay's direction. Then two riders entered the street from the east and caught their attention. As they tried to identify them, the women shielded their eyes from the morning sun. Clay took his chance. He pulled down the brim of his hat, dug his hands in his pockets and strode out across the street. He kept his eyes on the ground and expected someone to call out his name at every step.

Clay turned into an alley between the two buildings opposite. Out of sight of the street, Clay worked his way along past the back doors to the saloon. The kitchen door was open and the air was rich with the smell of potatoes frying in bacon fat. When Clay appeared, Nicolette stifled a scream. She frantically waved him away. He ducked round the corner of the building and heard Farrow's voice bark breakfast orders at her and the clash of plates and cutlery as she served up the food.

Inside the saloon, Pitch finished his breakfast and pushed aside his empty plate. He drained his cup and looked around for Farrow for a refill. The saloon was almost full. Farrow was frantic. Why had the cook gone sick on the day there was a wagon train in town?

Pitch lost patience. He stood up and rattled a knife on the edge of a cup for silence.

'Many of you townspeople volunteered to form a posse a couple of nights ago to ride out and bring in Clay Butterfield.'

Everyone in the saloon turned towards him.

'Justice couldn't be served on that occasion because the Regulators broke open the stable.'

There were grumbles from some of the men in the room.

'As your sheriff, it's my duty to protect this community by making sure that justice is done. I shall be calling for a posse a second time. I want Clay Butterfield brought in so he can stand trial for the murder of John and Amy Anderson and for the burnin' down of their farm. And this time, there will be a reward.'

'How much?' someone called.

'Only a few days ago,' Pitch continued, 'I purchased the Anderson property as independent agent for the Cumberland Mining Company. I dealt with John Anderson personally and he got the price he deserved.'

'Why did Anderson change his mind?' another voice called. 'He told me he wasn't never going to sell.'

'He was a businessman,' Pitch said. 'He knew what a good offer was.'

'What about the reward?' the first voice called again.

'It's become clear to me that John Anderson selling to the Cumberland could have been the cause of the argument between him and Butterfield,' Pitch said.

People turned to each other as they considered this.

'The reward is a hundred dollars for the bringing in of Clay Butterfield. I'm a generous man, I'll put up the money out of my own pocket as a gesture of good faith for you townsfolk.'

Nicolette stood in the kitchen doorway listening to this. The plate of eggs she was holding slipped from her hand and shattered on the floor.

'Look what you're doing,' Farrow snarled. 'There's customers waiting.'

As she knelt down and began to clear up the food and pieces of broken china, a buzz of conversation rose. Everyone had something to say about the sheriff's generosity. Then one of the men from the wagon train stood up. He was thin and his clothes were patched and worn through.

'You won't need no posse, Sheriff. I claim that reward. There's a fella hiding out in one of the wagons. I dunno his name but likely it's this Butterfield you're looking for.'

The man pointed at Roy.

'He's in his wagon right now.'

The man appealed to the other people from the wagons.

'No one wants a murderer on the train.'

Nicolette stood up with her hands full of eggshells and broken china and disappeared into the kitchen.

'He's mistaken, Sheriff,' Roy said. 'Ain't nobody travels in my wagon 'cept my wife and me.'

Pitch's Colt was in his hand.

'I need a posse right now to search the wagons.'

Everyone jumped to their feet.

Pitch marched out of the saloon and across the street with the man seeking the reward at his elbow. The saloon crowd surrounded the wagon. Pitch stood back from the tailboard.

'Burn him out,' one of the townsmen shouted.

Roy shouldered through the crowd and jumped up on to the wagon. He wrenched open the canvas awning and pulled it back. Pitch cocked his pistol. But there was only the usual pile of furniture and bedding.

'What did this fella look like?' Pitch said, holstering his gun.

The man described Clay.

'That's him,' Pitch said.

★ ★ ★

The wind was getting up again and the sky was darkening even though it was only the middle of the day. Rose Alice slid down off her horse and pulled herself up on to Nicolette's wagon. She gripped the shotgun tight. Everything was fastened down and neat, just as it always was. The supply box was full and the water barrel was untouched. They must be coming back. She pictured Nicolette's smiling face as she stared out over the empty land.

There was a tear in the canvas roof of the wagon. Nicolette couldn't have noticed it or one of them would have repaired it right away. If the wind kept up, it could rip the canvass in two. Rose Alice opened the supply box, helped herself to a piece of Nicolette's hard tack and forced herself to eat. The taste of flour and salt in her mouth sickened her.

Back on her horse, Rose Alice continued in the direction of town. She wished she had brought the piece of embroidered linen with her. She would have loved the feel of it at her throat now. She would have loved to run the tips of her fingers over the silk flowers.

Instead, she gripped the cold barrel of her gun.

The wind swirled around her, plucking at the blanket she wore over her clothes, pulling at her hat, trying to push her off course. One minute, the wind boxed her ears, the next it moaned in some far corner of the prairie and hurled clouds across the sky. Lightning forked on the horizon. In the distance, thunder rattled like gunfire.

And Rose Alice thought of Clay: Clay coaxing the fire alight in the freezing cabin, Clay trying to fix the shingles on the snow covered roof; Clay with his arms around her teaching her to use the shotgun when he could hardly shoot himself. She thought of him coming to look for her after he left the army and discovering her in the burned out barn. She thought of him buying a wedding license from the man who had passed by and told them he was a preacher.

Now somebody wanted to kill Clay and he had gone looking for them. She had tried to persuade him to run away but he had gone to make a stand for their new life, the one they were going to have in California where no one ever wore a coat and you only needed fires for cooking. He had gone to make sure they would be safe. She had to be with him. After all, if something happened to him, there would be no new life and she did not want the old one. Lightning forks stabbed the ground. Thunder rattled, closer this time. The wind carried rain.

13

The crowd melted away. Some made their way back to the saloon, others stayed with their wagons. Pitch scanned the street. If Butterfield had come back to town, what had he come back for? The man was a fool: that much was obvious. Black clouds moved over the town and rain fell. Thunder rolled somewhere out across the prairie.

As Pitch turned towards the saloon, his eye caught Zeke following someone into the bank at the far end of the street. Zeke was supposed to be upstairs at the saloon resting the leg he made so much fuss about, wasn't he? The other man entered the bank before Pitch could see who he was. He felt his Colt bump against his hip as he followed them to find out what was going on.

The bank was empty. There were two

grilles and a skinny clerk in an eyeshade stood behind one of them reading a newspaper. He looked up and greeted the sheriff as he walked in. Behind the counter, the door to the manager's office was open. Pitch could hear men's voices and see Zeke's back. He lifted the wooden flap at the end of the counter.

'Sheriff,' the clerk protested.

Pitch ignored him.

The manager was at his desk, Bill Choke was seated in front of him and Zeke stood at Choke's shoulder. The door to the safe was open a couple of inches and Zeke held a wad of twenties in his hand. The men turned towards Pitch. The smile fell from Zeke's face when he saw who it was.

'Two lawmen in the bank at the same time.' The manager beamed. 'You'd think we'd had a robbery.'

Nobody laughed.

'What's going on?' Pitch said.

'Why, Mr Choke has just made a withdrawal.' The manager sounded surprised.

Pitch stared at the bills in Zeke's hand and looked him in the eye.

'I pay your wages, not him.'

Choke started to get up out of his seat.

'Sheriff, I can explain.'

'This is bank business,' the manager said.

Zeke folded the bills in half and closed his fist round them.

'What are you sayin'?' Zeke said.

'You makin' deals behind my back?'

'Sheriff,' Choke protested. 'We was just — '

'Just what?' Pitch snarled.

He flicked back the side of his jacket and showed the pistol ready in its holster. The manager was on his feet now, calling for calm and reason.

'You makin' some kinda deal? You bribing an officer of the law?'

'No, Sheriff,' Choke said. 'It was just — '

'Just what?'

'Sheriff, I really think . . . ' the manager said.

'It was for protection,' Choke said.

Outside, thunder dynamited the sky. The building shook.

Zeke went for his gun then, but with his hand full of money, Pitch was too fast for him. Pitch fired and greenbacks scattered into the air like startled birds. Zeke clutched his arm. Pitch rounded on Bill Choke and shot him in the chest. Zeke flung himself through the door and ran out through the bank. The manager yelled in terror, raised his hands above his head and backed against the wall as Choke toppled over his desk like a tree.

'You saw him go for his gun,' Pitch barked.

The manager nodded, shaking with fear.

'They were in it together.'

Outside, bullets of rain drilled the muddy street. The surface of the puddles danced and the mud erupted in tiny splashes under the force of the storm. Rain beat on the wooden roofs of the buildings and drummed on the canvas of the covered wagons. It drove everyone inside and took control of the town. Pitch stood outside the bank with water dripping off the brim of his hat and surveyed the street. Zeke had disappeared. A bolt of lightning jagged across the sky and thunder exploded close by. At his feet, Pitch saw a trickle of Zeke's blood mixed with the mud and rain.

Pitch barged back through the bank and into the manager's office. The clerk with the eyeshade cowered beneath the counter. The manager was on his knees gathering up the twenties. He jumped up and raised his hands again. Choke's body was face down across the desk.

'The deeds,' Pitch snapped.

The manager backed towards the wall again, money sliding from his hand.

'Sheriff, I — '

'If Bill Choke had a mortgage, you got the deeds in the safe,' Pitch said.

The manager grabbed the back of his chair to stop himself from keeling over.

'A small . . . Yes he did. Bill had a mortgage.'

'Then you've got the deeds,' Pitch said. 'Hand them over.'

'I . . . ' the manager stammered. 'That's the property of the bank, Sheriff. I can't . . . '

Pitch cocked his gun.

The manager swung open the heavy door to the safe revealing a neat pile of documents. His hand shook as he passed over the deeds to Choke's property.

'This property is forfeit,' Pitch said.

'But Sheriff,' the manager said, 'the mortgage . . . '

Pitch tucked the document into his inside pocket and left the bank. Outside, the storm had started to ease.

In the saloon, Pitch took his usual table. No one else sat there since he had been appointed sheriff however busy the saloon was. Farrow joined him and waved to Nicolette who was serving the few remaining customers, to bring them coffee.

'Wagons will move out as soon as the rain stops,' Farrow said. 'Reckon we ought to search 'em again?'

Pitch outlined what had happened in the bank. Farrow shrugged.

'Got the deeds?' Farrow said.

'That's what I said.'

'Should be enough to keep Cumberland interested.'

Nicolette banged a coffee pot and two cups down on the table and flounced off without asking them if they wanted anything to eat.

'You'll have to ride over to the head office at Frankfort,' Pitch said. 'Tell them that if they give us a good price, we'll throw in the deeds to the other farm.'

'Butterfield's?'

'Up front payment for the exploration, up front payment for mining rights and monthly rent when they start to dig.'

'We ain't got Butterfield's deeds.'

Pitch laughed.

'If Butterfield is in town, I'll kill him.

213

If he's run off across the prairie, I'll get up a posse.'

Farrow sat back in his chair and contemplated his future wealth.

'What about Choke's wife?' Farrow said. 'She'll still be at his farm.'

'Tell Cumberland they can have vacant possession on all three properties. You do the negotiations. I'll see to things here.'

Farrow looked aside, unwilling to meet Pitch's stare.

'You best get going right now,' Pitch said, 'before Cumberland signs a deal somewhere else. If they see you right away, you could be back this time tomorrow.'

Farrow stood up and walked over to the window to inspect the sky.

'Rain's easing,' he said.

'The Cajun can work the saloon,' Pitch said. 'She ain't going nowhere. If Butterfield is here, he'll come to find her sooner or later.'

'I'll tell Sam to take charge of her,' Farrow said.

Pitch put the deeds to Bill Choke's place on the table in front of him.

'Anderson's deeds is in my office. We'll walk over together.'

*   *   *

With the stable door open, Zeke positioned himself in a pile of hay which gave him cover behind a stack of bales and a clear view of the street. He watched the men harness horses to the wagons. The animals were skittish after the downpour and the men whispered to them and tied nose-bags to their bridles to calm them. Further up the street, he saw Pitch and Farrow leave the saloon and hurry down to the sheriff's office. He drew his gun, inched back the hammer and laid it on the straw beside him. Minutes later, the men came out again. Pitch headed back to the saloon and Farrow walked towards the stable.

Zeke ducked behind a bale and grabbed his gun. He heard Farrow call for Sam and make some arrangement about him taking charge of the saloon for a while because Farrow had to ride to Frankfort on business. For a moment Zeke thought Sam might give him away. But Sam saddled Farrow's horse for him and watched him leave. Then without looking back at Zeke, he set off down the street towards the saloon.

Frankfort. Head Office of the Cumberland Mining Company. Right away, Zeke knew what they were doing. It was only a matter of time before Pitch came looking for him. He couldn't run because of his leg but Pitch's bullet had passed through the muscle in his arm. He could still shoot. He smiled grimly to himself: maybe Farrow would find Zeke York and not Eli Pitch as sheriff when he got back from Frankfort. He set his Colt down on the straw again. Pitch must have figured out where he was by now. Let him come.

Zeke heard rats rustle in the straw somewhere behind him. Then he felt the cold barrel of a .45 press into his neck at the same time as he heard the oiled snick of the gun being cocked just below his ear. Instinctively, his hand jerked towards his own gun, but a man's boot, split along the seam, kicked it away.

Keeping his Colt pressed into Zeke's neck, Clay Butterfield climbed over a hay bale, sat down and faced him.

'You packin' anything else?'

Zeke shook his head. Clay leaned over and patted him down. Then he sat back, still covering Zeke with his Colt.

'Should have taken up my offer,' Zeke said. 'I would have killed him for you. You wouldn't have this trouble now.'

'Ain't over yet,' Clay said. 'Besides, you ain't come out of this so well.'

Zeke's leg was stretched out in front of him. Blood had soaked through the leg of his pants. There was more blood on the sleeve of his jacket.

'Farrow's rode to Frankfort,' Zeke said. 'Means he's making a deal with Cumberland Mining. You know who's farm he's gonna sell.'

'Cumberland don't want my place,' Clay said. 'Not on its own.'

'Won't be on its own,' Zeke said. 'Choke's dead. You know what happened to Anderson.'

'Bill's dead?'

Zeke laughed bitterly.

'They took over damn near the whole valley. Only ones left is you and crazy Rose Alice.'

Clay shoved the Colt into Zeke's face.

'I warned you to mind your words before.'

'All right,' Zeke said. 'I didn't mean nothin' by it.'

Clay took the Colt away.

'What I'm sayin',' Zeke said, 'is that if you leave right now, he'll take your farm but he might not follow you. If you stay around, he'll take your farm and kill you sure as hell.'

'What's it to you?'

'You still got that hundred in the bank?'

'You think I'm giving you all the money I've got?'

'You've got a wife to stay alive for, ain't you?'

Outside, the storm had cleared the air and the day was bright. The men collected the feed bags and climbed up on to the wagons. The drivers flicked the reins and called out to the horses. The train lumbered forward. Nicolette stood in the doorway of the saloon and waved to Roy and Martine. Other townsfolk emerged from the buildings to watch the wagons leave. Pitch came out of the saloon and started down the street towards the livery stable. Zeke nodded in his direction.

'Gonna make a stand?' Zeke said.

'Something I got to do first.'

Clay got to his feet and slipped out of the stable by the back way.

Zeke kept his eyes on Pitch. On his way down the street, he stayed close to the buildings.

'Zeke, you in there?'

Pitch stood outside the stable to one

side of the door out of Zeke's line of sight.

'That was a misunderstanding,' Pitch continued. 'You hurt?'

Zeke reached down and retrieved his gun.

'You shot me. What do you think?'

'Listen I — '

'What do you want?'

'I didn't ought to have done that,' Pitch said. 'I thought you was selling me out.'

'Why would you think that?'

'We've rode together a long time,' Pitch said. 'The war. I lost everything. You know that.'

Zeke steadied his Colt on a hay bale and covered the open door.

'You've always been a cheat and a liar,' Zeke called. 'In the war you went back home, found your wife had taken your children and run off north. You burned your own house down and blamed it on the blue bellies. Told that lie so many times you believed it yourself. Set out in a whirlwind of murdering and burning till there wasn't no one safe. Now you've got it in your head to kill every man in that Yankee unit that rode through. War's ended and you're still killin'.'

'Never heard you object while you could make a profit by it,' Pitch said.

Zeke waited for Pitch to show himself at the open door. His finger was ready on the trigger. But there was no movement from outside, the street was empty and Pitch did not answer.

'You sold me out to Farrow,' Zeke called again. 'I know what's going on. He's rode off to Frankfort to do a deal with Cumberland.'

'You got it wrong,' Pitch called. 'When Farrow gets back from Frankfort, we'll all be rich men.'

Pitch's voice wasn't coming from the same place. Was he moving round the back of the stable? Zeke couldn't cover both doors from here. He strained to hear a footstep, anything that might give Pitch away. Silence filled the stable. Then there was shouting somewhere up the street. An argument erupted outside the saloon. Through the open door, Zeke saw a crowd had gathered.

'Eli,' Zeke called.

No answer.

Zeke forced himself up from behind the hay bale and stood in the middle of the stable trying to watch both doors at the same time.

'Eli?' Zeke called again. 'You there?'

The commotion outside the saloon had drawn more people out on to the street. It was hard to tell what was going on.

'Eli?'

No answer. Maybe he'd gone.

Holding his pistol ready, Zeke moved quietly to the back door of the stable and peered outside. Nothing. Just the sound of angry shouts somewhere up the street. He pushed the door. A hinge creaked. Still nothing. He glanced back into the stable. Grey afternoon light, the hay bale he'd hidden behind and the open front door, nothing more.

Zeke took a pace outside. Pitch stepped round the side of the building and, before Zeke had a chance to raise his weapon, shot him dead.

14

The ashen-faced clerk stared at Clay, and stammered something about fetching the manager.

'Tell him I want my hundred dollars,' Clay said, 'and you can close the account.'

There was shouting in the street outside. When the manager appeared, brushing down the front of his jacket in an effort to claim dignity in front of a customer, the clerk's eyes stayed riveted to Clay. The manager's hair was damp with sweat and he steadied himself on the edge of the counter. His hand trembled.

'Mr Butterfield?' the manager said.

The clerk kept his distance.

'My hundred dollars,' Clay said.

The disturbance in the street was louder now. The clerk peered out of a window. The manager mumbled something about a process and requiring a signature.

'I ain't got much time,' Clay said. 'I

need my money now.'

The manager disappeared into his office to the safe and came out with ten tens and a ledger. He pushed the bills across the counter and began to make an entry in the ledger to record the closure of Clay's account. The clerk lifted the counter flap and made for the door.

The manager's careful copperplate took too long. Clay stuffed the bills in his pocket and went over to the window. Sam Logan was holding Nicolette by the arm and trying to drag her down the street towards the sheriff's office. There was a heap of broken crockery at her feet. She was swinging punches and screaming curses while a crowd of spectators jeered encouragement and laughed out loud. She was getting the better of him. Inside the bank, the only sound was the scratch of the manager's steel nib against the page.

Then adrenaline jolted through Clay's veins. The bank clerk was running up the street pointing directly at the bank. Pitch was beside him, his Colt in his hand.

'Got a back entrance?'

Clay lifted the counter flap. The manager jumped back, dropping his pen. Black ink spattered over the perfect script. Clay shoved open the office door, looking for a way out. Bill Choke's body was slumped face down over the desk. A patch of blood had soaked through the back of his jacket. Instinctively, Clay placed his fingers beside Choke's neck to feel for a pulse and turned back to the manager.

'Who did this?'

Clay drew his gun. The manager squealed and held his hands up in surrender. Clay waved the barrel of his Colt.

'Sheriff.'

Clay checked the view of the street. Pitch and the clerk were right there. He dashed into the office again. No back door. He heard boots running up the wooden steps to the front door of the bank. He leapt up onto a chair, covered his face with his arms and hurled himself forward through the window behind the desk. Glass exploded round him. He took the fall on his shoulder, somersaulted forward and stumbled to his feet, head ringing, pain beating his bones. He ran. Forward. Away from the bank, down behind the row of buildings. He was aware of shouting from the street. He kept running. He had his gun in his hand, he knew that. He kept on. His heartbeats exploded in his chest. Every breath burst his lungs. On and on. Then there was the sound of gunshots. A bullet whined past him. Another tore splinters off the side of a building. Another kicked up a spurt of mud at his feet.

Then Clay was at the end of the street. There was nowhere else to go. He flung himself down behind the last building, his chest heaving. He peered back the way he had come. Pitch was at the far end of the street at the back of the bank. The clerk was beside him. Pitch was pointing his Colt, but Clay was way out of range now. Pitch took one last shot. The bullet sang but fell short.

Earlier.

'Mayor Farrow says I got to keep an eye on you.'

Sam Logan leaned in the doorway of the saloon kitchen.

Nicolette clashed a pile of plates together on the wooden table, filled a tin bath from a bucket of water and began rinsing them off.

'I don't know what's got into you,' Sam continued.

A plate slipped out of Nicolette's hand and shattered on the stone floor.

'Careful now,' Sam said. 'You know what Tom's like about breakages.'

Nicolette glared at him.

'Why don't you see if anyone wants serving at the bar?'

'I'll do that,' Sam said. 'While I do,

why don't you rustle me up something to eat?'

Nicolette turned back to the stack of plates. A minute later, Sam was back.

'I liked you,' Sam said. 'And Pierre. I just don't understand what happened. One minute you're getting along as nice as pie, the next Pierre's cheatin' at cards and shot the sheriff.'

Nicolette ignored him. She splashed a plate into the cold water and rubbed it clean.

'One minute you're workin' here, savin' every last dime for California, next thing Sheriff Pitch has thrown you in jail.'

'Sam, please.'

'It's that bad Cajun blood. Just rises up in you,' Sam said. 'I guess you can't help it. I feel real sorry for you.'

'You don't know what you're saying,' Nicolette said.

'Is there any eggs left?' Sam said.

'If you want something to eat, make it yourself.'

'See what I mean?' Sam said. 'A week

back you wouldn't have said that.'

'A week back . . . ' Nicolette began, then stopped herself. 'What was that?'

It sounded like a pistol shot. Then there was another. Somewhere in the direction of the bank.

'I'm staying inside,' Sam said. 'I ain't got a gun.'

Nicolette pushed past him and walked through the saloon. A group of men was crowded round the door. Across the street, the sheriff stepped out on to the porch of the bank. The men shrunk back from the doorway. Nicolette watched as Pitch walked down the wooden steps and headed down towards the livery stable. He looked neither right nor left. Nothing seemed to be wrong. Maybe they had misheard. The men went back to their tables and Sam joined them. Nicolette went back to her dishes.

Nicolette was up to her elbows in grease and cold water when Clay suddenly appeared at the kitchen door.

'I got to get across the street to the bank.'

Nicolette glanced into the saloon. Sam was sitting at a table with his back to the kitchen. Any moment now he would shout at her to bring him a cup of coffee.

'Can you get everyone's attention?' Clay said. 'So no one sees me.'

Nicolette looked at him. Quiet Clay, her husband's friend, who couldn't shoot and couldn't farm and spent his days dreaming of Californian sunshine. She sensed a new strength in him now. He was the only other person in town who understood what Pitch was like. Because there was no proof, no one would believe that Pitch had killed Parsons and her husband. But Clay would. He had dared to come back even when there was a price on his head. Clay smiled at her and was gone.

'Hey,' Sam shouted. 'There's men in here wantin' more coffee.'

Nicolette gathered the pile of china plates in her arms and walked through the door into the saloon. As she passed Sam's chair, she knocked his hat

231

forward over his face with her elbow.

'I quit,' she said. 'Make your own coffee.'

There were shouts, laughter and the sound of chairs scraping on the wooden floor behind her, but Nicolette didn't turn back. She strode out of the saloon, down the steps and stopped in the middle of the street. Exploding with fury, Sam ran after her with the men from the saloon right behind him. As she turned to face them, she saw Clay sprint across the top of the street to the bank. She let the pile of plates spill on to the ground where one after the other shattered in a hail of breaking china.

The crowd of men stopped dead. Then Sam let out a wounded roar and grabbed her by the arm. Nicolette tried to shake him off and when his grip bit into her arm she flailed punches and kicks at him.

'I'm takin' you back to jail and buryin' the key,' Sam yelled.

Keeping Nicolette at arm's length, he

started to drag her down the street. One hand held Nicolette and the other held his hat. The crowd of men roared with laughter. Some yelled encouragement to Sam, others to Nicolette. The sound of a pistol shot from the direction of the livery stable made everyone look up. The men retreated to the saloon. Sam continued to haul Nicolette in the direction of the sheriff's office.

When they got there, Sam shoved Nicolette into the cell and clanged the door shut. Where was the key? Sam rummaged through the desk drawers while Nicolette sat watching him.

'Tom Farrow's gonna blame me for those plates,' Sam blustered. 'What got into you?'

'Cajun blood,' Nicolette said. 'Ain't nothing I can do about it.'

Sam looked at her curiously.

'You should feel sorry for me.'

Nicolette noticed the bank clerk run past the office window down the street towards the stable.

'Now you're makin' sense again,'

Sam said. 'That bad blood ain't rising up no more.'

He slammed the desk drawer shut.

'Sheriff must have gone off with the keys. Think you can stay calm enough to work if I take you back to the saloon?'

Nicolette shook her head.

'Can't tell,' she said. 'That bad blood can rise up any time.'

Sam opened the cell door.

'Well you just tell me if you feel it risin' and I'll grab hold of you to stop you doing damage.'

Outside, the clerk and Sheriff Pitch ran past them in the direction of the bank. Sam was about to call out to him about the missing keys but saw that the sheriff was holding his gun. Just as Sam and Nicolette reached the saloon, Pitch and the clerk clattered up the wooden steps to the bank. There was the sound of a window being smashed and then a series of shots from a .45. Sam shoved Nicolette inside.

* * *

Clay's heart hammered in his chest. Would Pitch follow him? The stable was across the street. Hardly a safe place. If you stay around he'll take your farm and kill you sure as hell. Clay's horse was in the stable. No chance. Pitch wouldn't let him get away now. A picture of Rose Alice came into his head. He remembered how she didn't believe him that it would be warm all year round in California. He had to find some place to hide out at least until dark.

Clay pulled his hat down low, ran across the street and edged along the wall of the stable. The horses stamped and turned in their stalls. By the back door, Zeke's body was face down in the mud. Clay's throat dried. No point in feeling for a pulse. Zeke's gun was still in his hand. Clay glanced back but no one was following. He crept along behind the row of buildings looking for a place where he could get out of sight.

The old lean-to shed beside the hardware store would do. No one used it much and it was opposite the sheriff's office. Clay levered up a couple of boards from the back wall, squeezed inside and pulled the boards in place after him. Lines of daylight sliced between the rough planks and fell on a stack of new axes with smooth beech handles, their ironwork wrapped in brown wax paper. Beside them were four old wagon wheels with rusted rims and a pile of hessian sacks where a family of mice nested.

Hunkered down on the earth floor, Clay had a good view of the street through the cracks in the door and made himself as comfortable as he could. He checked the chamber of his Colt. Six shells. Daylight was beginning to fade and people were walking about in the street now. Pitch strolled past with the bank clerk beside him and went into the sheriff's office. Had he given up looking for him? When they came out, a few minutes later, the clerk was wearing a deputy's star on the lapel of his coat and had a .45 strapped to his hip. With his new deputy beside him, Pitch stood on the office porch and surveyed the street as though he owned it. Clay watched them. They were waiting for something.

Could take him right now, Clay thought. His gun felt cold in his hand. But the new deputy was beside the sheriff. Even if Clay did manage to shoot one of them, there was no chance he could take them both. It was still light, people were about and there was a price on his head. If neither the sheriff nor the deputy shot him, someone else would. He had to wait, had to pick his moment.

Outside the sheriff's office, Pitch consulted his pocket watch and men began to drift down the street from the saloon. Ma Parsons and some of the women emerged from the store and joined them. When a crowd had formed in front of the sheriff's office, Pitch started to speak.

'Now what I got to say ain't pretty,' Pitch announced. 'But as your sheriff, I got to tell you that there's been some shootings. My deputy Zachariah York was killed right behind the livery stable. Now there's only one person who could have done that. Zeke was doing his duty by searching for Clay Butterfield. He must have come across him and . . . '

Pitch spread his arms. He didn't need to tell them who had done it. People in the crowd turned to each other.

'There was also a shooting at the bank. Your neighbour Bill Choke was shot dead.'

Pitch held up his hand for silence.

'Butterfield was seen running away from the bank. I followed him. I took some shots at him, but like the snake he is, he slipped out of range.'

Pitch paused. He searched the faces of the crowd.

'Now, I can't protect you all single handed. I've appointed a new deputy and I'm gonna double the reward for

Clay Butterfield but I need you townspeople to step up. I want you to keep your guns close by your sides this evening. I want you to watch out. If he don't show himself tonight, every last one of us will search the town in the morning.'

A buggy driven by a woman appeared at the eastern end of the street and trotted past. The grim faced crowd turned to stare at her. Ma Parsons recognized the woman and called out. Dark clouds massed in the sky. It was going to be a night without a moon.

★　★　★

Clay pulled his jacket around him. The cold air stiffened his joints and froze his bones. A mouse scuffled somewhere close. One by one, pools of yellow light from the oil lamps lit the windows while torches blazed on each side of the saloon door. When the undertaker's cart had made its last journey, the street was empty. Clay had seen Pitch head for the saloon and leave the new deputy inside the sheriff's office an hour ago. Clay had a good view of him drawing and redrawing his Colt in front of a mirror.

Hunger clawed in Clay's belly. Maybe it was safe to slip up to the saloon kitchen to get Nicolette to give him some food. He still didn't have a plan. How could he confront Pitch without being gunned down? How could he convince the people of the town that he was innocent? Some of these people had known him all his life. All it had taken was the word of a new sheriff and the promise of a hundred dollars for them to turn against him. Don't think about that. Let them think what they like. All that matters is to stop Pitch coming after him and to get back to Rose Alice alive.

An east wind got up. It blew down from the mountains, across foothills and the open prairie. It chilled the muddy surface of the street until it was crisp with ice. It curled between the buildings and cut through the frail walls of the shed. Clay hugged his arms around him. He crawled back to loosen the planks so he could make it to the saloon kitchen. Then he heard hoof beats at the end of the street.

Through the cracks in the door, Clay saw a rider wrapped in a blanket dismount outside the sheriff's office. The deputy, still watching himself in the mirror, looked startled as the rider pushed open the door. The rider's back was towards the window. The deputy was shaking his head and saying something. He was appealing to him. It looked like some sort of argument. Then the deputy raised his hands and spun round to face the wall. Clay could see a shotgun barrel sticking out from under the blanket. The rider grabbed the deputy's .45 out of his holster. The deputy had his hands behind his back and the rider was handcuffing him. Then the rider opened the door, shoved the deputy at gunpoint out into the street and pushed him in the direction of the saloon. Each time the deputy hesitated, the rider jabbed him with the shotgun.

Lit by the flickering torchlight as they approached the saloon, the blanket fell away from the rider's face. Clay kicked open the door to the shed and ran towards them.

'Rose Alice,' he shouted. 'What are you doing?'

15

Rose Alice forced the deputy into the saloon. A pool of nicotine lamplight covered each of the tables. The smell of tobacco and sour whiskey thickened the air. Sam and Nicolette stood behind the bar; Pitch occupied his usual table next to the stove. Ma Parsons sat with a group of women and the remaining tables were taken by Euchre players. There was a storm of conversation. At first, no one looked up.

The blanket fell from Rose Alice's shoulders. She wore Clay's old saddle jacket and had the deputy's gun tucked in her belt. She blasted one of the barrels into the ceiling. The place froze.

'I got something to say,' Rose Alice said. 'In case you don't know me, my name is Rose Alice Butterfield.'

She jabbed the barrel of the shotgun into the back of the deputy's neck. He whimpered softly.

'And don't you think I wouldn't blow his head off. Because I would.'

Rose Alice started to tell how Zeke came out to the farm and told them there was someone in town who wanted Clay dead.

'Clay didn't believe him,' she said. 'You know Clay. He ain't done an unkind thing in his life.'

She told them how it was connected to the war, something the 23rd had done.

'Jim was in the 23rd,' Ma Parsons called out.

Ellen Choke was sitting beside her.

'And Bill,' she said. 'And John Anderson.'

The room was breathless. Everyone was thinking the same thing. Parsons, Choke, Anderson: they were all dead.

'Now, I don't know who this man is who wants to kill Clay. But I reckon he's in town right now.'

Pitch got to his feet.

'You got it backwards, ma'am. I got

to tell you, your husband is wanted for murder. There's a price on his head.'

Rose Alice jabbed the shotgun into the deputy's neck.

'Clay never killed nobody. He ain't got it in him.'

'Put the shotgun down,' Pitch said.

'Why are you wearin' that star?' Rose Alice said. 'Where's Sheriff Parsons?'

Someone sobbed at the table where the women were sitting.

'Zeke wanted Clay to give him a hundred dollars and the deeds to the farm,' Rose Alice continued. 'He said he'd kill the man for him.'

'He said the same thing to Bill.' It was Ellen Choke's voice. 'Only he asked for a thousand. Bill beat him down. He came into town to get five hundred out of the bank.'

Everyone turned towards her.

'Well, who was it?' Sam called out from behind the bar. 'Who was comin' to kill them?'

There was a silence while everyone looked into the women's faces. Then

Pitch started to laugh. And the crowd, which had started to believe the women and started to think that Clay Butterfield was wrongly accused, was confused again. They looked at Rose Alice and remembered that everyone said she was crazy; they looked at good natured, loyal Ma Parsons who would never countenance a bad word against her husband; they looked at Ellen Choke who had driven her buggy into town to look for Bill and found him dead. They had almost believed the story but before they were convinced they had to have proof and there was none. Pitch's laugh hung in the air as dry as smoke.

'I know who it was.'

Everyone turned to the back of the room.

'It was him.'

Nicolette pointed at Pitch.

'He killed my husband too.'

Sam grabbed her arm.

'What did I tell you?' he hissed at her.

Conversation broke out in the room then. Pitch was ready to round on Nicolette, but there was no need. He could hear it in everyone's voices. That was just the Cajun talking. No need to pay attention. He smiled indulgently at her and turned back to Rose Alice.

'Ma'am, I'm asking you real nice,' Pitch said. 'Just put down that scatter-gun.'

'There's a murderer here,' Rose Alice said. 'No one's doing nothing about it.'

Pitch heard desperation in her voice. He pushed towards her between the tables. Up close, he gestured to her to hand over the gun, but Rose Alice kept it pressed against the deputy's neck. Staring straight ahead, the deputy was shaking now and tears welled in his eyes.

'Where's Tom Farrow?' someone called. 'He's the mayor. Let him decide.'

'Gone to Frankfort,' Pitch said. 'Won't be back till tomorrow.'

As he spoke, Pitch reached in his

holster with his right hand and pulled the shotgun away from the deputy's neck with his left. Everyone heard the metallic snick as Pitch cocked his .45 and pointed it at Rose Alice's face. But she wasn't looking at the Colt, she was staring at the hand which had wrenched the shotgun away from her. 'Where did you lose them fingers, Sheriff?' she said.

Hatred flickered in Pitch's eyes. He shoved her aside and holstered his .45. He turned his back on her and walked back to his seat, still holding the shotgun.

The flames in all the lamps flickered as the saloon door swept open. Clay stood there.

The crowd shrunk back to the walls leaving an open corridor between him and Pitch. Pitch turned and the shotgun clattered to the floor.

'I got somethin' I want you to hear,' Clay said.

Pitch's hand rested on the handle of his Colt.

Clay pulled the bank manager into

the saloon and stood behind him.

'Tell 'em,' Clay said. 'What you told me.'

'I . . . '

'You got some nerve,' Pitch snarled. 'There's a price on your head. You ain't gonna get out of here alive.'

'Tell 'em,' Clay repeated.

'I . . . '

The manager was shaking.

'Tell 'em who killed Bill Choke and why.'

He looked at Pitch.

'I can't, I . . . '

'Yes you can.' Ellen Choke was on her feet. 'You've known Bill and me for years. Good times and bad. If you know something, tell it now.'

The manager looked at her.

'Bill withdrew a sum of money and paid it to the deputy, Mr York. That's all it was.'

'How much?' Ellen Choke said.

'Five hundred dollars.'

'I told you Bill beat him down,' Ellen Choke said.

'What else?' Clay said.

'That's all it was.'

'After the money, what happened?'

The manager stared at the floor.

'There was shootin'. Sheriff came in and said the deputy was takin' a bribe and Bill was payin'.'

The manager hesitated.

'Wasn't the sheriff's fault. The deputy was armed and if he was breakin' the law — '

'You're sayin', the sheriff shot his deputy?' Clay said.

'Only winged 'im. He ran off somewhere.'

'What about Choke?'

'Died straight off. Sheriff caught him bribing an officer of the law. That's what he said.'

A pistol shot cracked and Clay was catapulted backwards. The saloon erupted. Amidst terrified shouts, everyone flung themselves out of the way. Rose Alice hurled herself forward and made a grab for the shotgun at Pitch's feet. Pitch looked down, kicked the gun aside and it skidded away under the tables. A second shot blasted. Clay's gun was in his hand. Pitch reeled and his pistol dropped to the floor. He looked surprised as he ran his hand across the patch of blood on his shirt and sank back on to a chair, his face the colour of snow. Rose Alice grabbed the shotgun and stood over him.

'Where did you lose them fingers?'

Pitch looked confused.

'In the war,' he said. 'Some Yankee girl came at me with a hatchet.'

He clutched the wound in his side. Blood ran through his fingers.

'That was me,' Rose Alice said. 'For what you done. You burned my house. You killed everyone in it. That was my folks.'

Clay struggled to his feet, still gripping his .45. His left arm hung useless at his side. Blood drenched the sleeve of his jacket and dripped on to the floor.

'Did you hear him, Clay?' she said.

'He's the one that did it.'

Clay walked towards her to put his arm round her.

Pitch made a grab for his .45 and swung it towards Rose Alice. Clay saw him and fired. And fired again. And again and again until the chamber was empty. At such close range each shot hit Pitch in the chest. His body crashed backwards, through tables, into the bar.

Clay drew Rose Alice to him and held her tight.

It took time for the room to recover. No one spoke. Eventually there was the sound of people struggling back to their feet, picking up chairs and righting tables. Clay and Rose Alice stood holding each other while the saloon reformed around them. Nicolette came from behind the bar and embraced them both.

'Clay came back when he could have kept on running,' Rose Alice said. 'He did it for the both of us. I had to stand with him.'

Clay held her close.

'You gave me a reason,' he said.

'One guy makes a stand then others follow,' Nicolette said. 'Look at these people. They're right behind you now.'

Clay looked round the saloon. Everyone's eyes were on him.

'You come right over to the store and let me and Ellen take a look at that arm,' Ma Parsons called.

The crowd stayed in the saloon. No one wanted to be the first to leave. By staying there they showed they were grateful to Clay and that they knew they had been wrong. They sat respectfully at their tables, the packs of cards piled in front of them, their glasses drained. Nicolette started to sweep up broken glass into a tin pan. The everyday sound of her brush on the floorboards was the sound of the town being put right again.

Pain stiffened Clay's face as Rose Alice helped him towards the door. Ma Parsons and Ellen Choke led the way. As the four of them went out into the street, conversation rose in the saloon. Outside, the wind had died and the night was still. The clouds shifted and moonlight cast the town in silver. Ice crackled under their feet and their breath hung in clouds in front of their faces.

In the room behind the store, a black iron stove threw out heat. Ma Parsons filled a pot of coffee while Ellen Choke cut away Clay's blood-soaked sleeve. A splinter of white bone stabbed through the flesh of his upper arm. Clay gasped and gripped Rose Alice's hand like a vice.

'Fetch the whiskey bottle, Ma,' Ellen said.

It took an hour. Clay bit on a leather strap while Ellen doused the wound in whiskey and aligned the broken bone. Ma bound it tight with torn up sheets and splints made from pieces of a crate from the store.

'My Bill should have stood with you, Clay,' Ellen Choke said. 'He told me you came to see him.'

Clay lay on the couch. His bandaged

arm rested on cushions. Rose Alice sat beside him.

'After the war, he didn't want to leave the farm,' Ellen Choke continued. 'He just wanted to work and make the place prosper. He said he'd take care of the farm and the rest of the world could take care of itself.'

Ma Parsons rested her hand lightly on Ellen's shoulder.

'The mining company made us a good offer,' Ellen continued. 'Bill wouldn't have none of it. He said this was farming country. I guess I'll have to sell out now. I can't run the place on my own.'

'Stay with me until you do,' Ma Parsons said.

'Our deeds are with the bank,' Ellen said. 'Bill took out a mortgage when he came home from the army. What he'd saved out of his army pay wasn't enough to get the farm started again.'

'Quit worrying about that until the morning,' Ma Parsons said. 'The bank will let you call an end to the mortgage.

You and Bill have been customers all these years.'

Clay's eyes were closed and his breathing was light and regular. Rose Alice felt his grip loosen on her hand.

'You can sleep in a chair right beside him,' Ma Parsons said. 'I'll build up the fire.'

16

Sunlight warmed the air as Tom Farrow rode into town the following afternoon. There was no one about. He searched for Eli Pitch in the sheriff's office and the saloon and ended up at the store. Clay was still resting in the back room, being looked after by Ellen Choke. Rose Alice and Nicolette had ridden out that morning to check on the wagons.

'I ain't stayin',' Farrow said. 'I came to tell Sheriff Pitch that we were too late. Cumberland Mining have bought land rights a hundred miles east. They ain't interested in land round here no more.'

Farrow took two folded documents from inside his jacket and put them on the table. Ellen Choke caught her breath.

'This one's the deeds to our place,'

she said. 'Bill never would have parted with this.'

'Sheriff told me he acquired yours and the Anderson deeds,' Farrow said. 'I thought you and Bill must have agreed to sell.'

Ellen Choke stared at him.

'Did you ask?'

Farrow's face was stone.

'If mining came here the whole town would be rich. You, me everyone.' Farrow said. 'But now, it's just going to roll on as a farm town.'

'Maybe that's what folks want,' Ellen said.

'Not me,' Farrow said. 'The president of Cumberland Mining saw me walk into his office holding two sets of deeds and he offered me a job as a staff negotiator right off. Salary plus commission. There ain't enough money for me in a farm town saloon. I'll sell it to the bank. They'll find someone to take it on.'

'You can leave the Anderson deeds with me,' Ellen said. 'John would have wanted that.'

Clay lay on the couch with a blanket over him. Colour had returned to his face. Ellen Choke smiled at him.

'You still set on leaving, Clay? There's a lot of land here that wants managing.'

'I want a new life,' Clay said. 'One where Rose Alice and me can make a fresh start. Soon as I've got my strength back we'll be heading west.'

'Got enough money to last you?'

'A hundred dollars. We'll drive to Missouri and pick up passengers there. That should cover the passage. Nicolette will do the same. If it comes to it, we'll sell one of the wagons.'

Ellen opened the door to the stove and fed in another log. The flames roared in the chimney.

'Rose Alice up to the journey?' she said. 'The girl's as thin as a wand.'

'We're strong if we're together,' Clay said.

'Guess the whole town will be hopin' you'll change your mind,' Ellen said. 'I will too.'

'Make me an offer for the saloon,' Farrow said. 'I'll give you generous terms.'

Clay shook his head.

'You could get Sam to help you and the Cajun girl. She's a hard worker.'

'We want a new life in a new place,' Clay said.

'You think on it,' Farrow said. He glanced down at the two parchment documents which lay on the table as he turned to go. Ellen Choke placed her hand flat down on them.

'Goodbye Tom,' she said.

Farrow touched his hat.

'Bill never trusted him,' Ellen Choke said after Farrow had gone. 'Always said he was out for what he could get.'

The fire crackled. Ellen got Clay to lean forward while she plumped up the cushions behind him.

'We're going to miss you, Clay,' Ellen said. 'Did you see the way everyone was looking at you in the saloon? The whole town knows you championed them.'

Clay settled back on to the cushions

and let the heat from the stove soak into him.

'I told Rose Alice there's sunshine every day in California and you never have to light a fire except for cooking,' he said. 'Do you reckon that's true?'

Just as the afternoon light was beginning to fade, Rose Alice drove her wagon into town. Nicolette sat beside her. It would take some time for Clay to be fit enough for the journey and they could tend the chickens and the goat if the wagon was close by. They had decided to bring in Nicolette's wagon the following day. They talked about picking up work at the saloon while they waited for Clay to recover. Farrow was delighted and hired them both right away. He pressed Rose Alice to get Clay to consider a tenancy.

Rose Alice was never happier. Clay was recovering, she spent her days with Nicolette and California was on the horizon. Nicolette showed her the daily routine of cleaning at the saloon. Rose Alice relished the work and even

Farrow was surprised at how good the place looked. Nicolette herself helped the cook and tended bar with Sam when Farrow was away. Cumberland Mining business took him on increasingly frequent trips out of town. The bank placed an advertisement for a saloon manager in the *Frankfort News*.

★ ★ ★

Over the next month, the stream of visitors wore Clay out as he lay on the couch in Ma Parson's parlour. Some of them were people he had known for years, others he knew by sight, more were strangers. All of them came to thank him and all of them urged him to stay. When he told them about his plans, everyone had advice about the journey. Some of them brought him presents: there were parcels of hard tack wrapped in cloth, an Indian knife, a lucky horseshoe, a handful of shotgun shells and a cotton shirt.

Ellen Choke decided to take up Ma

Parsons' offer and move in. She drove her buggy out to the farm to collect Otto and the possessions she needed and hired two men from the saloon to board up the house. Farrow approached Cumberland Mining again on her behalf to see if they would reconsider an offer for the farm but they were committed in the east of the state. With the bank acting as her agent, an advertisement for the property was placed in the Frankfort press.

After four weeks, Clay's arm was still in splints but his strength had returned. He was anxious to leave. There had been no further snow and the ground was softening. He estimated that it would be frozen four inches below the surface out on the prairie. The going was still good.

The two wagons slipped out of town one morning as a blood red sunrise divided the earth from the purple sky. Sam Logan stood in the doorway of the livery stable and watched them leave.

'Aim for that. Keep going straight,'

he called. 'There ain't nothing between you and Independence.'

Rose Alice clicked her tongue and shook the reins. The wagon lumbered forward.

Nicolette's wagon followed.

'Want to know what they asked me last night?' Clay said.

Rose Alice looked at him.

'Sam and the bank manager and some guys from the saloon came round while you were loading up.'

Clay stared ahead into the brightening day.

'They said if I would consider stayin', they'd make me sheriff of Vengeance.'

'And what did you say?'

Clay moved close and put his good arm round Rose Alice's shoulder.

'Can't help you, fellas. Rose Alice and me is off to California.'